The Purpose

of

Prudence de Vere

Patsy Trench

A Roaring Twenties novel

Prefab Publications

Published in 2019
by Prefab Publications, London

Prefab Publications, London

ISBN 978-0-9934537-4-8

§

While this book is a work of fiction a number of real and recognisably famous people appear in it. Their lives and their personalities have been researched carefully, but any interaction they are supposed to have had with the (fictional) Prudence De Vere or her (fictional) friends and family is, of course, entirely invented.

'The person without a purpose is like
a ship without a rudder.'

Thomas Carlyle

§

'"Would you tell me, please, which way I ought
to go from here?" asked Alice.
"That depends a good deal on where you
want to get to," said the Cat.
"I don't much care where," said Alice.
"Then it doesn't matter which way you go," said the Cat.'

Lewis Carroll, *Alice in Wonderland*

Introduction

London, 1926

Anyone who knows me will be astounded to hear I have written a book. I am fond of boasting I have never even *read* a book, in fact I have been known to pour scorn on the whole world of literature.

However this memoir is the result of a challenge. My friend and companion Dougie McAvoy and I were arguing over dinner about writers, and writing in general. I told him I divided the world into two: the doers, and the commentators. The conversation went like this:

'The people who really have something to write *about* are very rarely the people with the time to write about it,' I said.

'So you're saying you are too busy to write your story?' he responded.

'I have better things to fill my day with.'

'Or are you really implying you don't have anything to write about?'

A word of explanation is needed here.

I have a reputation, which I have not discouraged, of what used to be known as a good time girl. It's true I have had adventures of the romantic kind, many adventures, but I have also, as you will discover if you care to read my book through, done very much more. I have dallied with actors and cavorted with suffragists. I have been on intimate terms with the Bloomsbury group and toyed with the spiritualist world. I have befriended some remarkable people, many of whom you will recognise. One way or another, though I say it myself, I have led what I consider to be an extraordinary life.

'I believe I have had an unusually interesting life,' I said to Dougie. 'Just because fact is so often far stranger than fiction doesn't mean it isn't fact in the first place.'

'Very well.' He threw down the gauntlet. Or more precisely, his knife and his fork. 'Do it. Write your story. See if anyone will believe it.'

'All right, I will.'

'I bet you won't.'

'Why do you say that?'

'Because writing books is hard work. You need to closet yourself away from the world, from people, from life altogether, for long periods of time.'

'Ha! A couple of hours a day is all it needs. I'll have it done in no time.'

'All right.' Dougie reached out his hand and I took it and shook it firmly. 'I'll give you a thousand pounds if you complete it in six months. And if you don't, I will do it for you.'

Now I would never call myself mercenary, but that was a challenge I could not resist. A thousand pounds to someone like Dougie is a serious matter.

To be honest I did not think I would manage it, I've never been one for hard work. But it's funny, once you start to think back over your life it becomes kind of addictive. After six months I'd finished what Dougie rather pompously called my 'first draft', which he then went over, correcting my grammar and spelling mistakes and turning what he described as my scribbled notes into readable prose.

And he paid his debt, and we celebrated at the Ritz, several times.

So here it is. The unexpurgated tale of my extraordinary life.

Prudence de Vere

1

I have no idea what my parents had in mind when they had me christened.

What's in a name? Well, in my case, everything. Nobody walks around with a name like Prudence and pretends it doesn't matter. I was ten years old the first time somebody laughed in my face when I was introduced. He was a boy not that much older than me and when I asked him what was so funny he tapped the side of his nose – a ridiculous habit he'd obviously picked up from some adult somewhere – and said, 'Prudence is as Prudence does.' When I asked my father later what he was talking about, he laughed. That was all.

It was typical of my parents that they never explained anything to me. If I say I was ignored as a child you will feel sorry for me and that wouldn't do at all. But my mother was absent-minded enough to leave me behind in the Princess Angelina nursing home after giving birth. It wasn't until the maternity nurse arrived on our doorstep several hours later, with this wee thing in a bundle, that Mama realised she'd completely forgotten about me.

I didn't see much of my parents as a child. I was looked after from the start by a nanny, and later by whatever maid happened to be around, or more often than not, nobody. There is a story my brother told me once about how I was minding my own business in my bedroom one day when this woman poked her nose around the door. When I asked, 'Who are you?' she replied, 'I'm your mother.'

That more or less set the tone for the rest of my life. It was the same for my older brother Toby (now *he* was given a perfectly ordinary name). Unusually for offspring born at that time – 1875 in my case, 1871 in Toby's, in the reign of our great Queen Victoria and all that that implied – the two of us were left alone for much of the time. Meals were a bit hit and miss, so for the most part we just raided the larder whenever we felt hungry. There was usually some leftover chicken or ham, and with a bit of luck some apple pie or even, joy of joys, treacle tart. It's a wonder we didn't become grossly fat.

Looking back, I suppose it was Toby's job to look after me, he being six when I was two and so on. He bullied me, of course, as older brothers do. He called me *mop-top*. I was a skinny little thing then, believe it or not, and even at that young age I had this hair that I could do nothing with. He told me horrible stories that gave me nightmares. He used to prod me and poke me as if I was a doll. It took a while before I learned to answer back, and from then on my life was what you might call transformed. It was my first important lesson in the skill of survival.

What education we had, Toby and me, was mostly done by a young woman called Sybil, who came to our house twice a week and taught us reading and sums and later on history, after a fashion. The teaching took place in little snippets, in between the gossip. She was a great one for gossip, was Sybil, and I realise now that she had the most tremendous imagination. I think I learned more from her stories than I ever did from her teaching. They were mostly about her neighbours. There was a Mr Snitch, who wore a pince-nez and used to squeeze her cheek in a highly annoying manner. Sybil said that behind closed doors he was 'a master of the Dark Arts', whatever they might have been, and could turn toads into cats and vice versa. Opposite him lived Mrs Barnstaff, who may or may not have been a spy, and who used to peer through her curtain whenever she saw Mr Snitch leave his house. It was she who told Sybil about the Dark Arts. Mrs Barnstaff had a Mr Barnstaff who Sybil said was horribly henpecked. In my innocence I wondered why he allowed himself to be pecked by hens, in fact why he kept hens in the first place if they pecked him.

It was Sybil who told me about my name. 'Prudence means caution,' she said. 'And good judgement. Always thinking before you leap, that sort of thing.' She had a tendency to mix her mottoes.

Well. That acted like a red rag to a bull. In fact you could say it was those words, along with the other quirks of my upbringing, that shaped me, that made me who I am.

Invisible parents, a brother who bullied me, and my name.

I could have turned out very differently. But you make the most of what God, or life, throws at you. Don't you? And I don't regret a thing.

2

It was Sybil too who taught me about sex. I was about eight years old at the time and I had no idea what she was talking about then, but it was useful information to store away until later. She used to talk about 'doing it', sometimes with a friend called Jimmy, and sometimes with Terence. There were others too, but they were too fleeting to remember. She used to 'do it' in all sorts of places, in bathrooms, once on someone's Persian rug, and sometimes in the open air. When I asked her to explain 'doing it' she blushed, and went all coy, and said I was far too young. But there was one day, when Toby was elsewhere, that she clasped her hands together on the table, glanced around to see if we were being overheard and then: 'Very well,' she said. 'It's like this.'

And she told me.

My face must have been a picture because she looked at me and laughed out loud.

I mean, what a peculiar thing to do. It sounded really awkward, not to say painful, and what on earth was the point of it all?

'It's how people make babies,' she said, and gave me a sweet smile.

'So do you have lots of babies?'

'No. Not yet.'

'So it doesn't work?'

'Thank the Lord.'

'Why do you thank the Lord?'

'Because I'm not ready to have babies and besides, not with any of them.'

'Then what is the point of it, if it doesn't work, and why do you do it with them if you're not ready to do it with them?'

Poor woman. She must have regretted ever saying anything. But she just laughed again in her merry way and gave me a little hug, which came as a shock as hugs weren't part of our daily lives back then. She said there was a lot more to it than what she'd made out, and that when it came to it I would understand what she was getting at. And while at the time I was totally confused, she was right. When I did eventually come to 'doing it' I understood completely.

How lucky that it was Sybil who taught me about the birds and bees and not my mother. Or anyone else. Because it was Sybil, fun-loving, promiscuous Sybil, whose attitude to that fascinating topic again shaped my own. Sex, she was trying to tell me, even though its primary aim was to produce babies, could be enjoyed for its own sake, even with people with names like Terence with whom she had very little conversation, but who in her words was a terrific lover and had a fine body.

I'll never forget Sybil. She was possibly the single most important influence in my life, and I'd like her to know that.

~

When I was thirteen years old my brother went off to join a firm of accountants as an apprentice and I was left completely to my own devices. Sybil left soon afterwards, I never did discover why, but presumed it was because one of her adventures with one of the young men she 'did it' with had been successful. It wasn't the reason however:

I learned later my parents didn't think it was worth spending any more money on educating their daughter once my brother was gone.

I spent long days on my own, wandering the streets, talking to people and swimming in the lake in Regent's Park, which was quite close to where we lived in Clerkenwell. On the third occasion I was greeted on emerging from the water by a large policeman, my towel in his hands. When I asked him what he was doing, he said he was about to ask me the very same question. Did I know I was contravening not one but two by-laws of the Royal Parks: swimming in the lake and not wearing a bathing suit? When I asked him in return how a person was supposed to know about by-laws when there were no notices to be seen, he responded that most people with a head on their shoulders – an odd expression I thought then, since how would a person be able to walk around without one? – would not need a notice to tell them what anyone with an ounce of common sense already knew.

That was how I learned things. Lacking any other form of instruction, or as I see it now, restriction, I did what I wanted and learned, perhaps the hard way, what was and was not acceptable. It is a method I highly recommend as one is never hidebound by what some may term 'proper behaviour', imposed for the sake of some mystical idea of what is done or not done, otherwise known as snobbery.

~

This being the time of the chaperoned female, the sight of a girl wandering the streets of London on her own attracted a bit of attention, needless to say. I was even, more than once, accosted by a policeman asking why I wasn't at school or at home. I started out by saying I was an orphan, with no home, but I quickly realised this was a Mistake and meant I would be carted off to the nearest workhouse. So despite the temptation to say things like I had set out with the express purpose of getting to chat to a policeman – also a Mistake, as joking with policemen is a total waste of time I soon discovered – I had to resort to mundane excuses such as my mother was ill and she had sent me out to buy some milk, which also got me into hot water when the policeman insisted on escorting me to the nearest grocer and watching while I stood there like an idiot mumbling that I had forgotten to bring any money.

So my wanderings continued, to the West End, and it was here that two important things happened: I lost my virginity, and I fell in love. I was around sixteen at the time though I pretended to be older.

The virginity went to a boy called Mikey, who used to lurk round the back of the Adelphi Theatre in the Strand. He called himself the stage doorkeeper but he wasn't, he was a stagehand of some kind, and part-time at that.

He had bright red hair and freckles, and he was as skinny as a rake. But it was his voice that did it for me. It was the purest Cockney I had ever heard and it made me swoon with lust. He really did use words like 'ain't', and 'gor blimey', expressions I had thought belonged only in fiction. In return he called me la-di-da and told me I had a plum in my mouth. It was the first time anyone had drawn attention to what I later discovered to be known as 'class'.

It's not really fair to say that Mikey took advantage of me because I was, as the saying goes, ripe for the plucking. It began as a series of fondles backstage, behind what he called the 'legs', and I can remember to this day the feeling of his hands on my naked thighs. The first time we 'did it' was in a dressing room, late one night when everyone else had gone home and the caretaker had locked up, thinking the building was empty. It was a disaster, as these things inevitably are. But by early the next morning at attempt number four or five we were beginning to get the hang of it. I can't say it was enjoyable but, a bit like the first cigarette of the day, once you've got over the initial nausea it starts to feel not quite so bad.

But then something else happened inside that building, something altogether more life-changing. I fell in love. Though not, you will be unsurprised to hear, with Mikey.

3

On cold days Mikey would let me come inside the theatre and hang around in the warmth. We'd chat over cups of tea, or if there was no one else there we'd 'do it' round the back of the scenery dock. Better still, I would get to sit in the Dress Circle of the auditorium and watch the men building sets. The stench of the paint was terrible but otherwise it wasn't a bad way of passing a few hours.

One morning a tall spindly creature in a straw hat appeared on the side of the stage and stood there for several minutes, while nobody took the slightest notice. Eventually a man in shirtsleeves went over to her and they had what looked to me like an altercation, though I couldn't hear a word they were saying over the banging and crashing of the stage crew. After a few minutes, during which she became increasingly agitated, the woman stormed off the stage in what might have been tears.

I had quite forgotten all about this until some days later when Mikey managed to sneak me into a performance during the interval through the pass door. Having missed the first half of the play I had very little idea what was going on, but it did seem to me to be rather silly – what they called a melodrama. It took me some time to realise that the utterly gorgeous creature standing on the stage beneath the lights, this nymph, so slight she was almost not there, was the same gangly creature I had seen arguing with the shirtsleeved man several days before.

Now I've never understood the point of plays frankly. This business of actors walking out on a stage and talking in a loud voice to nobody in particular is too artificial for words. But that evening changed everything. That was the evening I fell in love.

I believe I startled the rest of the audience by leaping to my feet at the curtain call and shouting 'Bravo!', because that was not what was done in the theatre in the '90s, not even at the Adelphi. I didn't think twice about presenting myself immediately at her dressing room door, tapping loudly and hearing her call out, 'Come.'

She was sitting at her dressing table gazing blankly into the mirror. She was still dressed in her stage clothes, a skimpy black number that accentuated her frailness, and her still-made-up face in the reflection of the harsh lights made her look quite unreal. I wanted to touch her to see if she existed, but instead I stood behind her chair for some time before she appeared to notice me. At which point, without really looking at me, she said, 'Do I know you?'

'No,' I said. 'My name's Prudence.'

There was a small pause before she smiled slightly and said, 'And are you?'

I ignored this. I'd heard every joke there was to hear about my name. I just said, or blurted out rather, 'I just wanted to tell you I think you are – glorious.' It sounded ridiculous then and it sounds even more ridiculous now, but it was sincerely meant.

She looked at me briefly and away again. 'Thank you, darling,' she said. It was the first time anyone had called me darling and it made my heart leap almost right out of its socket. 'I'm glad someone thinks so.'

She pulled at a wad of cotton wool, tore open the top of a large tub of cream and proceeded to smear the stuff all over her face. She rubbed at it with such violence it was as if she was trying to obliterate herself.

'I hope you're not thinking of entering this profession darling, because if you are, think again.' She snatched at another dollop of cream and scrubbed away at her eyes. 'They are nothing other than charlatans and back-stabbers, it's a profession fit only for madmen.'

When I didn't immediately reply she swivelled in her chair and looked right at me. The make-up around her eyes, smudged by the cream, made her look like something you might meet on a dark night at Hallowe'en.

'Then why did you choose it?' I ventured, quite bravely in the circumstances.

It was an obvious question but it seemed to take her by surprise. She swivelled back to face the mirror and said, savagely, 'I was given the sack today. They told me my performance is below par, that I have a "weak voice" and "feeble gestures". Two weeks' notice. And all because of their execrable play, and the abominable notices. I am the scapegoat.'

'So what are you going to do?'

She stared at her reflection. 'Kill myself maybe.'

'Oh! But you can't – you mustn't!'

She laughed. 'I am not serious. Well, not really.'

By now the make-up was gone and there was her face, naked and shiny, and I felt at that moment an overwhelming sense of protectiveness. I wanted to wrap her in my arms and hold her to me. This woman, this girl – she could not have been more than a few years older than me – this unearthly creature, opening herself up to a complete stranger. Oh, glorious indeed!

'Perhaps I can help you,' I found myself saying.

'Help me? How?'

'I could be your assistant, or your dresser.'

She got up from her chair and went over to a corner of

the room and proceeded to remove her costume. There was no self-consciousness; it was as if I was her oldest and most intimate friend.

'I couldn't afford to pay you, darling. Anyway, there's nothing to assist me with, let alone dress me in, if I'm out of work.'

She stood stock still for a moment, in the shadows, in her undergarments, looking like a lonely little child.

'You won't be out of work for long. I guarantee it.'

One does say the stupidest things when one is young. But to her credit she just smiled, and as she pulled her dress down from its hanger she looked at me and said, 'What a strange creature you are. Where did you spring from?'

I was about to tell her about Mikey but quickly realised she was not looking for a literal answer.

'You dear thing,' she said. 'Dear, odd-looking thing. Hook me up, would you?'

So I did, with trembling fingers, fumbling, her body so close to me I could barely breathe.

She spoke more softly then. 'I do it for my children,' she said, 'and for my mother and for my husband. So that we all may eat.'

'You're married?' I tried and failed to keep the panic from my voice. I don't know what I was thinking really, or expecting, but hooks done, she turned around and gave me a pat on the cheek.

'He's a long way away, in Africa, I've not seen him for six years. His health is even worse than mine and he struggles, more than me even.' She gave me a wan smile.

'Do you love him?' I cried. I was fighting for breath.

'Oh yes,' she said gently. 'Passionately.'

She laughed out loud then and before I knew what she was doing she drew me to her and gave me a hug. It was only the second hug I had ever received in my life, after

Sybil's, and as hugs go it was not effusive. It was more like hugging an object than a person, she was so boned and corseted. And the hug said, which she did not, 'Don't be disappointed.' And it was over.

~

I tried to keep away from her after that. I thought she might not be such a good thing to have in my life, what with her airs and her superiority. Besides, she had been sacked which meant she was a failure and I didn't want to associate myself with failures. Why should I?

Nonetheless a week later I found myself back in the theatre again. I was hanging around in the wings with Mikey, trying to keep out of the way of the crew, but she saw me and raised an eyebrow and whispered, 'You again,' before she swept onto the stage. Watching from the wings I found myself once again mesmerised. I tried to fight it. I tried to leave, but something – she – kept pulling me back. I was darting hither and thither like a demented pigeon straining to see as much as I could without obstructing the entrances and exits of her fellow actors. One of them, old enough to be my father, gave me a wink and a tap on the backside just before he made his entrance onto the stage playing, suitably enough, a villain. As he came off stage later he murmured something in my ear which I chose not to hear, as even then I knew I was being propositioned and I didn't want to have to tell him, 'You are wasting your time, I am in love with someone else. I am in love with *her*.' Because it was true, I was, I really believed I was.

A week later she was still there. It appears she had been offered a leading role in a new play at another theatre and the management, suddenly and almost too late deciding that if she was wanted elsewhere then she was wanted here also, had withdrawn their notice. So she muttered to me as she made her final exit from the stage,

'Perhaps you would like to work for me after all, since it appears I am not completely on the scrap heap.'

The play closed soon after that, and not a day too soon, said Stella. We were on first-name terms by then, or rather I refused to call her by her stage name of Mrs Patrick Campbell, as I could see no reason why a woman should be known by her husband's name when her husband was first, absent and second, apparently incapable of making enough money to support her. Stella found all this highly amusing and muttered something to the effect that it helped to keep his presence alive and that much closer to her, which remark made me all but throw up right there on the spot.

4

After the play closed Stella went straight into rehearsals for the new one. It was being presented at the St James's Theatre off Piccadilly, which even I could see was a cut or two above the lowly environs of the Adelphi. She was very nervous. She confessed to me, secretly, that this was the test that would prove to one and all, and not least to herself, whether or not she could act.

The play was another melodrama. It seemed to me, watching rehearsals, that it was not so very different from the mediocre rubbish she'd been forced to perform at the Adelphi. The story concerned a woman with a 'past', who married a well-to-do gentleman called Aubrey Tanqueray, but who for reasons which at that stage in my life were outside my understanding was never 'accepted'. So in the end she killed herself. There was a daughter involved – his, not hers – who let the cat out of the bag when she announced she was about to marry a man whom her stepmother Mrs Tanqueray had 'known' in her previous life. Which was, as Stella explained, the catalyst for Mrs T's suicide.

It was yet another example of theatre misrepresenting real life, in that it was all people shouting at one another unnecessarily, and women swooning and clutching their foreheads and crying out, 'Oh my dear!' in a way no normal mortal person ever did, or not in my admittedly

22

limited experience. Granted, I could see this play contained elements of everyday life that might be recognisable to some people, and moreover, as Stella was at pains to explain to me, the writer, a Mr Pinero, was trying to make a serious point.

'About what?'

'About hypocrisy in modern-day society.'

'But nobody ever behaved like that. Why did she have to commit suicide?'

'Because she had a past.' Stella heaved a sigh, but I ignored it and ploughed on.

'What do you mean, a past?'

'She was a courtesan. That was her profession. She was trying to put all that behind her. She had fallen in love, truly in love, and she believed that she could forget her past and start a new life, only it turned out she was wrong.'

'What's a courtesan?'

'A courtesan is a high-class prostitute.' She was irritated now.

'And what . . .'

'Don't tell me you don't know what a prostitute is.'

'Is it someone who "does it" all the time with different men?'

That made her laugh, and forget for a moment her irritation. It was something I was able to do, to lighten things, to nudge her out of her moods, and she knew it.

The first dress rehearsal was for the benefit of Mr Pinero only. Mr Pinero obviously worshipped the ground Stella walked on, which was utterly understandable of course, except that he was a happily married man and it seemed his wife was no less smitten than he was.

She said afterwards, did Stella, that he'd been pleased, delighted even, and that there were tears in his eyes. I thought that was not just highly unlikely but, bearing in mind he was the author, frankly arrogant. Fortunately I had the wit not to say as much. Instead, from the deepest recesses of my unworldly heart I said, 'Well, I think you are the most marvellous actress in the world, and a simply miraculous human being,' which looking back is one of the moments one would most like to forget. But she had the grace to smile and give me a kiss on the cheek and to say, 'Thank you, Toffeehead, that is exactly what I wanted to hear.'

I meant it, of course, I meant it with all my being. But a bit of me, a large bit of me, still thought the whole theatre world was nothing more than histrionics. Take for example the practice of addressing other people as 'darling', not just because nobody can remember your name, but because since *everything* is heightened, *nothing* means anything, and *nobody* knows whether someone is being sincere or not. It was a distrustful business, the theatre; it was manipulative and unreal and I refused to be taken in.

But then I watched her, as the tragic Mrs Tanqueray. Again, from the wings. There were multiple changes of costume, some of them done very swiftly in a little corner offstage (if people think theatre is glamorous they only have to take a peek behind the scenes). To my utter embarrassment I found myself with tears streaming down my cheeks. When she killed herself I was inconsolable, despite telling myself – 'It isn't real, it doesn't make any sense, it's only a play. Killing herself isn't necessary, it isn't even logical. Nothing here bears any resemblance to real life, nothing at all.'

'Oh my darling girl,' she said to me afterwards. 'Are you all right?'

I thought I'd managed to mask the tears but evidently not. 'Just a bit of a sniffle,' I gulped.

'Were you moved, my darling?' She was still in her Mrs

Tanqueray clothes, in her dressing room, and she took both my hands in hers.

I sniffed. I needed to blow my nose but I didn't want to let go of her hands.

'Even you? Suspicious, sceptical you? So scornful, so reticent . . .'

'Reticent?' I wasn't having that.

'You know what I mean. Dearest Toffeehead, if I can move you, I can move mountains.'

I wasn't sure how much of a compliment that was meant to be, but I just shrugged. And then I cried a little, and then I allowed myself to cry a lot, and then laughed, and she laughed with me and gave me another hug, and I don't think I was ever so happy in my entire life.

~

Over the next few weeks Stella's fame grew, along with the accompanying adulation. She scoffed, to begin with, but I could see she was pleased. It was that very play, *The Second Mrs Tanqueray*, that turned Stella Campbell, better known as Mrs Patrick Campbell, into a star. Suddenly the town was lit up, with her at the centre of it. There were glowing reviews in the newspapers and the whole world turned out to see her. I was rushed off my feet, fielding callers and struggling to organise her social calendar. Mrs Pat had become the toast of the town, and the toast is expected not just to move mountains eight times a week, but to appear at functions and balls and dinners and who knows what. I watched her growing increasingly exhausted. And all she really wanted to do was go home to her children – or so she said – though the attention made her glow from the inside, I could see that better than anyone.

She wanted me with her, all the time. She insisted. And because they were glamorous events she had to do a rush job smartening me up. She bought me dresses, she hired a hairdresser to tame my hair, and she almost succeeded. 'You don't know how lucky you are,' she said to me on one occasion, 'not being a beauty.' She sighed. 'Fortunately you have other resources to get you through.'

I wasn't sure what she meant by that. I had never thought of myself as a beauty but that didn't mean I wanted it pointed out to me quite so bluntly. I must have pulled a face because again she took hold of my cheek with her fingers and gave it a playful squeeze and said, 'But you can make people laugh. That is a true talent, and never forget it.'

Over time the adulation got to her. She started to believe it. And the more she believed it the less she confided in me. It was as if she no longer needed a confidante. She was beginning to leave me behind – mousy, tousled-haired, odd-looking Prudence Brooks, otherwise known as Toffeehead, by Stella only, mind. I no longer fitted into her world. I could see it coming before she did, but that didn't lessen the shock of meeting my replacement one afternoon before the matinee.

'This is Josephine,' she said. That was all. Josephine was everything I was not. She was tall and elegant, and if not quite a beauty she had a grace I had never managed to acquire, not then and not ever. She exuded sophistication, and class, all the things that were beyond me. Whether or not she could make people laugh in the way I apparently could was beside the point. I had been supplanted.

Stella gave me what I took to be a rueful look and said, 'I'll miss you, Toffeehead.' And I knew, like everything else in theatre, that it was a lie.

There was something else Stella taught me, though she didn't know it. I could not reconcile the picture of the miserable wraith that I'd watched all those weeks ago standing at the side of the stage, ignored, with the creature who commanded centre stage, the eyes of a thousand people on her, as Stella, Mrs Tanqueray, went to pieces before our eyes. It's what's known in the business as star quality, and I wanted it. No, I didn't want to be standing centre stage, or anywhere else on a stage for that matter, God forbid. But in the theatre of life, if I can use a metaphor, I did not want to be that slight figure standing looking on while nobody paid her the smallest notice. I wanted to be the star. And that, you could say, was both the saving of me and my downfall.

~

For some time after that I became unbearable. I was still smarting at my sacking – as there's no doubt that was what it was – but no matter how hard I tried I could not bring myself to think badly of my darling Stella. Had she dropped me a line to apologise and offered to take me back into her bosom I would have gone like a shot, no questions asked. But thank God she didn't. I kept my dignity, insofar as I ever had any.

But I had moved, if only for a brief moment, among the cream of society of London, and though I scorned it while I was there I missed it when I was not. By contrast, everything and everyone who belonged to normal daily life seemed like shadows, not worthy of my attention. I yawned my way through the day, I made a point of ignoring everything my parents did and said. I thought I was going to die of boredom. I lost interest in Mikey – poor soul, he must have wondered what had become of me. All of it faded before the memory of those few months with Stella.

Fortunately I had the sense not to hound her at the stage door of whatever theatre she was appearing in, or to try to contact her in any way. *Mrs Tanqueray* ran for just under a year and her next production, *The Masqueraders*, which followed immediately afterwards, was a disaster. The newspapers sliced her into little bits, described her as 'inert', declared that 'the most talked about actress of the day would not, or could not, understand one of the most beautiful, complex, and subtle studies of women that any dramatist has offered us in the whole range of the modern drama.' (*Daily Telegraph*, 30 April 1894). I had to think about that one long and hard. I had to ask myself whether I was secretly pleased or distressed on her behalf. In fact I had to question the whole meaning of love – for there was no question, it was love. Was it a selfish thing? If one was spurned by the object of one's love, did one rejoice at her downfall? And if so, was that not simply revenge?

No. I realised that despite everything that had happened, those notices hurt me as profoundly as if they were aimed at me. I was Stella. I was Mrs Patrick Campbell. I knew true love.

I was grateful to Stella for another thing. If she couldn't transform me into a beauty overnight she could at least turn me into a reasonably presentable young woman. Even my mother remarked on it. Or rather, she gave me a look when I came down to breakfast one morning as if to say, 'Who is this?'

She taught me something else too, did Stella. She taught me about courage in adversity. Her life had not been a bed of roses. I learned she'd been so gravely ill at one stage she thought she was going to die. And there she was on her own, with her children, and her (useless) husband overseas and unable to keep his own body and soul together, let alone his wife and children's. Yet she pulled through and she battled on, and triumphed, all with a smile on her face. Because whatever you or I or anyone else says about the theatre, with its artifice and its bright lights and people pretending, it is not an easy life. There are predators out there just waiting for an opportunity to tear you to shreds, to raise you up one moment and bring you down the next, all on a whim.

5

At the ripe old age of twenty-four my brother Toby, who I had thought incapable of normal human emotion, announced his engagement to a young woman called Lucia.

Having fallen in love himself he became suddenly evangelical about the whole heady business and wanted everyone around him, his sister included, to do the same. To this end, he explained, he was anxious to introduce me to Lucia's brother Sacha, who was 'awfully handsome. Not that I expect for a moment he'd have you,' he felt compelled to add.

As anyone with a brother, particularly one as obnoxious as Toby, will agree, one will go to the ends of the earth to avoid consorting with anyone who is acquainted with him. In this instance, however, having offered up such an irresistible challenge I was intrigued enough to agree to meet this Sacha at least.

My brother's description was, for once, not an exaggeration. Sacha – a Russian name, he was quick to explain, and a total affectation, as was his sister's, since there was no trace of either Russian or Italian blood in the family – had the face of an angel, with dancing grey-green eyes and golden curls that cascaded almost to his shoulders.

I knew there was something not quite right when he

began flirting with me the moment we met. I know my limitations. I was even more sure of it when, on our first dinner engagement – only the second time we had met – he spent the entire evening talking about a writer called Oscar Wilde, whom he idolised; and who was even then, as he spoke, in the midst of a torrid court case in which he was suing some jumped-up minor aristocrat for labelling him a 'sodomite'.

Now I happened to know what a sodomite was. It was yet another useful life tip I'd picked up from my months with Stella. I had noticed one of the older actors in the company taking what seemed to me to be an unusually keen interest in one of the younger actors, and when I mentioned this to Stella she laughed and said, 'This is the theatre darling, it's what happens.'

'It's where what happens?' I asked, obtusely.

I was combing her hair between performances. She loved it when I did that. There was a lot of it, it was long and thick and lustrous and curled naturally – not in a frenzy, like mine – and it felt like velvet between my fingers. She would lean back in her chair and close her eyes, and she told me once there was almost nothing in the world so wonderful as having someone comb her hair. Someone, mark, not necessarily me.

'You'll soon get used to it, if you decide to pursue a career in this ridiculous profession.'

'Do you mean men doing it with men?'

She smiled. 'If you want to put it like that.'

I was fascinated. Even Sybil did not tell me about this.

'How exactly do they do it?' I asked.

'My goodness.' She opened her eyes and stared at me in the mirror. 'You are bold my dear, for a young one.'

But she answered my question, in some detail, more than I was expecting to be honest. I pulled a face, which made her laugh, and she told me they were known as queers.

'Why queers?'

'Oh darling, I've no idea. You'll have to look in a dictionary. Not that I suppose you'll find it in the Oxford, or in any other for that matter.'

'Do you think it's queer?'

She said she didn't think it at all queer, not in her experience. Unusual perhaps, and certainly not legal. 'But in the end darling, it's none of our business what other people get up in the privacy of their bedrooms. So long as they don't do it in the street and frighten the horses.'

'Are you queer?'

I was back with Sacha, in the restaurant.

His face lit up. 'Yes, I am! Are you?' He gazed at me expectantly.

It was a good question, and I wasn't at all sure how to answer it, as to tell the truth I hadn't yet sorted myself out in that respect. There had only been Stella in my life, and yet even I was beginning to realise that may have been more of an infatuation. The idea of 'doing it' with her filled me with horror. And yet the only person I had done it with at that stage was Mikey, and that only because he was a genuine Cockney, and he was very good at doing it, and he liked me because of my poshness. I don't suppose we exchanged more than a couple of hundred words together in the whole of our acquaintance. And yet here was a man, a complete stranger, to whom I felt I could say pretty well anything I liked, but who was out of the question so far as that side of things was concerned. I was entirely confused.

I told Sacha about Stella. He listened with shining eyes, leaning across the table towards me, drinking in every word and occasionally murmuring, 'Marvellous, oh top hole, utterly divine, love it,' which made him sound quite theatrical. 'Dear girl,' he said, when I was done, 'what a wonderful story.'

He told me then he'd had aspirations to 'tread the boards' as he put it, but his parents wouldn't hear of it, declaring that the world of theatre was full of rogues and vagabonds and queers. 'Heaven!' he sighed, and for a fleeting moment he looked quite mournful. 'It's the only place a person like me can be – a person like me, do you see?'

'Not really,' I said.

'Why do you think Oscar is having to endure all these shenanigans? Why do you suppose he's being put through the wringer? Have you thought about that?'

I didn't want to tell him I had no idea who Oscar Wilde was so I shrugged and said nothing.

'To be called a sodomite, in public, a man like that.'

'It's not a very nice word,' I acquiesced.

'Slander. Absolute slander.'

'You mean it isn't true?'

'Yes! No! Who knows? What does a man's private life have to do with anything, or anybody?'

'So long as he doesn't do it in the streets and frighten the horses,' I ventured.

'Oh, wonderful! Did you just think of that?' He clapped his hands in delight, and I didn't have the heart to tell him where the remark actually came from.

And I never really did get to answer the question about my sexual preferences. But I had made a true chum, somebody I could say anything and everything to. Dearest Sacha.

~

Sacha suffered from what he called 'an anxiety of existence'. Ever since he'd given up God, he said, he had struggled to find something else that gave his life structure and purpose.

I thought this was terribly grown-up and terrifically

intellectual. I had never given a thought to anything as deep as the meaning of life, but ever since Sacha brought it up I began thinking about it.

I could see it in other people. Stella for instance had purpose, a very real purpose even in her unreal world. Her purpose, acting, was given structure by the jobs she was offered, which didn't necessarily always bring her happiness as she was a Great Complainer and was always having arguments with the management. That got me thinking even more, that having something to complain about might fit the description of purpose, so in that respect I was well covered.

I looked to my parents but I couldn't see a lot of purpose there. My father's work kept him out of the house from early morning to late evening, which meant he was far too tired for anything else. My mother organised the house, after a fashion, and went for walks and had tea with friends, which she said was enough to fill her day. Whether or not that counted as purpose I'm not sure – Sacha didn't seem impressed.

I took to travelling round the streets of London on buses – on the top deck if the day was warm enough, as you got such a splendid view into the neighbours' front rooms and back gardens – looking for people with purpose and structure. I thought I spotted one, a middle-aged woman with a shopping bag who was walking so fast she almost collided with the lampposts, but then it occurred to me I was just mistaking speed for purpose. I observed an old man with one leg proceeding down the street at a snail's pace, and as he got to the corner he paused to catch his breath, and I thought for a moment that *he* had a very definite purpose, which was to get from one end of the street to the other. That got me thinking that purpose might have something to do with overcoming something, an obstacle or obstruction or, in this case, the man's disability. Which led me to wonder if Sacha's problem, and perhaps mine, if I had one, was *not* having an obstacle to overcome.

Sacha nodded gravely when I told him my thoughts. 'Yes,' he agreed, 'there is something in your theory. It's freedom of choice that is the difficulty. The oppressed, the lame, the homeless, the starving – it's very well for *them*!' he cried. 'All they have to think about is getting through the day, or proceeding one step closer to overthrowing the regime. If *that* isn't purpose I don't know what is. And yet,' he agonised, 'where are we without freedom?'

I was surprised, at moments like these, that Sacha wanted to spend so much of his time with someone like me. I was hardly his intellectual equal. When he went off on one of his rants I would sit there and let him get on with it, throwing in the odd remark now and again such as that if he really wanted to be homeless and starving it could surely be arranged, which threw him into a complete fury. 'That's not the *point!* It's not something you can contrive!' he would expostulate. So for the most part I just kept my mouth shut.

We used to spend a lot of time together in those days, maybe because we didn't have much else to do, either of us. We'd stroll through parks together or sit in tea rooms for hours until the waitresses gave us dark looks. 'I wish I could be more like you, Rudi,' Sacha told me one day. He called me Prudi for a while till he dropped the 'p' as Rudi was a boy's name, he explained, rather obscurely. 'Drifting through life without a care in the world or a thought in your head.'

I told him that was presumptuous and really quite rude. I said I had suffered as much as the next man, or woman, I just didn't go on about it or try to give it a meaning. Insofar as I had come to any conclusions about life, I went on, it was that things happened, for no particular reason that I could think of, and that looking for purpose was a waste of time. Unless, that is, you thought the purpose of life was looking for a purpose, in which case woe betide you if you ever found one. Sacha laughed and called me a philosopher. I told him if he could look inside my brain he would find an empty house with no furniture, but the more stupid things I said the wiser he thought I was, so in the end I gave up.

6

It was Sacha who introduced me to Claudia and her chums. They were a group of gay young things who met up at odd weekends at the house of one or other of their families, usually in Hampshire or Wiltshire or thereabouts, and preferably when the older generation were elsewhere. There would be tennis and swimming in summer, and croquet and cards, and shooting for the men in winter, and there didn't seem to be much purpose or structure to anything they did other than having fun, which suited me down to the ground.

I didn't take to Claudia to begin with. I found her aloof, even haughty, often just watching silently rather than joining in the conversations. I assumed that either she didn't have a thought in her head, or she knew she was so beautiful she didn't need to do anything other than sit there like a darned goddess looking down on her minions.

She was striking, I admit. It was hard to take your eyes off her, with her luminous hair and the biggest grey eyes you ever saw, looking out at the world warily from her perfect face. Naturally she was the centre of attention, especially among the men, but among the women too; yours truly excepted, of course.

On about our fourth or fifth meeting however she said something to me that took me by total surprise.

'I envy you,' is what she said.

'*You* envy *me*?' I exclaimed. 'Whatever for?'

'You have such an easy way with people.' She spoke so softly you had to bend towards her to hear what she was saying, which I thought was quite a clever ruse, if it was a ruse, which in retrospect I don't suppose it was. 'You make people laugh, you're fun, you're unafraid. I would give anything to be like that.'

Well, that changed things a bit, as you can imagine. It never occurred to me that anyone would envy a person like me, with my frizzy hair and my freckles, five foot nothing and growing stouter by the day. She went on to explain that she was shy, which was a word I'd come upon but never fully grasped. It meant, as I take it, that she was nervous meeting strangers, or when in company with more than one or two people.

I laughed, and told her that with looks like mine, I had to have some way of drawing attention to myself. It was a basic necessity. I was born like that, it was the only way I could remind my parents of my existence. She thought I was joking and laughed hilariously, hiding her mouth behind her hand as if she was being vulgar, which of course was a physical impossibility for someone like Claudia.

So a friendship was forged. There's nothing like mutual envy, and admiration, to glue people together. As time went on we became confidantes. We even shared gentlemen friends, or rather we took them in turns. Or rather, if I'm being honest, I would be approached by some young man who would spend time chatting me up before asking me, quite brazenly, if I could put in a good word for him with Claudia. You can imagine what I had to say to that. But after a while I got used to it, and actually I quite liked being the go-between and the recipient of her cast-offs, or her never-quite-got-theres. It did occur to me that in some ways they maybe preferred my company. I was less daunting, they could relax and enjoy a laugh with me, as chums, and sometimes it developed into something more and sometimes it didn't. I managed to have a huge amount of fun, and a lot else besides. And in between times there was always Sacha, dear Sacha. I think I probably loved him more than I ever loved anyone. More than Stella even.

You'd think Sacha would be a fish out of water in that kind of mindless *milieu*, but actually he seemed to rather enjoy it. He naturally drew the attention of the women, he was so beautiful, and gracious, and once they'd twigged he was absolutely no threat they took to him even more. And I have to say he didn't mind this at all – my dear, vain friend. The men were more wary, as you can imagine, although one or two also took a shine to him, with obvious consequences.

There was one member of the group who used to hang around Claudia more than the others. His name was Gerald and he was a total black sheep. The rest of us were empty-headed flibbertigibbets. There was a kind of unspoken rule that conversations never touched on anything too serious, or if they did, not for too long. We were out to have fun, to flirt and misbehave and get up to all sorts. But not Gerald. He only ever wanted to talk politics (*verboten*) or business (likewise) or ancient history, about which actually he could be quite interesting, though I tended to lose consciousness after the second paragraph.

There could be only one reason why he stuck around, and that was Claudia. Anyone with eyes could see he was besotted – except, oddly enough, Claudia herself. He didn't paw her as the other men did, or sit at her feet gazing adoringly up into her face and fiddling with the hem of her skirt as if it was the garment of a goddess. But you could see it in his expression. In a group it was as if none of the rest of us existed, and wherever Claudia went, he was right there. For her part she didn't seem to pay him much attention, even to be aware of his presence, which is why what happened subsequently came as such a surprise to us all.

By contrast Dougie fitted into the scene like a hand into a glove. He arrived one late-summer afternoon. He immediately reminded me of the actor Gerald du Maurier – suave, dapper, terribly (and falsely) self-deprecatory, with a permanent twinkle in his eye so you had no idea if he was being serious. He was a hit from the very beginning, especially with the women. He obviously preferred female company, he made that perfectly clear, and complained bitterly when he was dragged off on a shoot, where he disgraced himself by nearly taking out the eye of one of the beaters, at which point he was allowed to retire gracefully.

There were rules among this set, not written down, or spoken of, but sort of naturally absorbed. Nothing too serious, or too long-lasting, and that applied to relationships as well as conversation. Four weeks, six at the most, after which a man was supposed to at least propose to a girl, and if she didn't accept him then they could carry on regardless so long as they kept within the group and didn't try to sneak off on their own too often. Everyone had to keep within the group. No one gossiped outside the group. If a newcomer broke one of these rules, deliberately or otherwise, he was politely ostracised, and if he didn't correct his behaviour he would be invited to depart the scene – implicitly, of course, no one would be so vulgar as to openly send someone packing.

It was like one long cocktail party, a waltz, everyone on the move, changing partners, forming brief attachments and moving on, and if you didn't like it then you didn't have to put up with it.

7

I was strolling the streets of London again wondering what I ought to do with my life – not in the Sacha sense, you understand, it was a rather more practical consideration to do with it being time I earned some money – when I decided to pay a visit to my old friend Stella.

She was playing at the Garrick Theatre, yet another melodrama from the fine pen of Mr Pinero, by the name of *The Notorious Mrs Ebbsmith*.

It wasn't like the old days when I was able to go right up to her door and knock and enter; not at all. There was an entire phalanx of fearsome-looking men who greeted me at the stage door like guards, demanding to know who I was, what was my business there and did I have an appointment. I told them my business was a social call to my old friend Stella, otherwise known as Mrs Pat, and if they would care to inform her of my presence she would surely send for me immediately.

It didn't work quite like that. It was between shows and she was 'resting' they said, so I plonked myself down on a chair right by the stage door and said I would stay put until she was ready to see me. Ten minutes later I got the call and there I was, back in her dressing room with the same old Stella.

She greeted me with delight. 'It's my old friend

Toffeehead!' and pulled me to her bosom and laughed and then held me from her and gazed into my face for an age, saying things like, 'Oh my goodness,' and, 'My word,' and, 'Look at you' and other such nonsense. Then she sat me down and beamed at me for a full minute.

'So, my dear girl, how are you?'

'I'm fine,' I told her. She looked different, however. Older, and tired.

I told her of my exploits trying to run the gauntlet of the Mafia downstairs, and she sighed and said, 'Yes, it's ridiculous, isn't it.' And with another great sigh, which sounded exaggerated and theatrical and really quite affected, she went on, 'Things have changed somewhat, Toffeehead, since your day.'

'Oh, how come?'

'They think I need protection.' She was gazing despondently at her reflection in the dressing-table mirror, like a tragic queen. 'Who from, I've no idea. Not from the likes of you, obviously, but I suppose they cannot take chances.'

At that point there came a knock on the door and a stern-looking woman entered. She hesitated on seeing me and Stella said, 'Not yet, Gloria, come back in ten minutes,' at which point the woman called Gloria gave me a look that would turn a weaker person to water before withdrawing.

'That was Gloria,' said Stella unnecessarily. She placed her elbows on her crowded dressing table, knocking over a couple of pots, and continued scrutinising herself in the mirror. 'She's my dresser.'

'Oh? What happened to – whatsername?'

'Josephine?' Stella laughed shortly. 'She lasted a week. The woman had no idea, she found the whole thing quite beneath her. She had a cousin who was a duchess, I believe, and she clearly thought I was the one who should be looking after her and making her cups of tea and so on.'

I was confused. 'Why didn't you tell me? I would have come back, despite . . .'

'Despite?' Stella cocked her head on one side and frowned. I felt like a small child being humoured by a maiden aunt.

'Why didn't you tell me?'

She turned her gaze from me for a moment and blew through her lips and said, 'I didn't know where to find you, darling.'

This was so obviously untrue it was laughable. But I didn't laugh.

'So you've got Gloria instead.'

'I have Gloria instead.' She sighed again.

'And is she any better?'

I hadn't gone there looking for a job, but now the conversation had somehow turned to dressers it seemed a good opportunity. I'd seen Gloria for less than a minute but I'd immediately sensed the tension between the two women. There was an opening here, if I could just phrase it right.

Then Stella changed her tone along with the subject and, almost bouncing with eagerness she said, 'Tell me all about you, darling. What are you up to these days?'

'Not much,' I said, with a shrug.

'Are you married?'

'God, no.' It came out stronger than I intended, and she pulled a face.

I don't know why, but I felt awkward. Maybe it was because in her presence I found myself slipping back to the days of *Mrs Tanqueray*, which was only a couple of years before but seemed like a lifetime ago. Once again I felt like a gawky child in her presence, something that never happened with anyone else. It was highly uncomfortable.

'What about you?' I ventured.

'Me?' she said, as if she was surprised to be asked. 'Oh well, you know, ups and downs. Always busy.'

'Always busy.' I nodded wisely.

She smiled. 'Mr Pinero again, not such a well-written piece I'm sorry to say, although he does write such wonderful parts for women. I *love* the role of Agnes, though I quite disagree with the ending, we've had countless arguments about it. Some people say it is the finest piece of acting they have ever seen on a stage.'

I looked to check if there was humour in this last remark but I couldn't see any. She was not the woman I used to know and love.

'So, is Gloria a good dresser?'

'Dear me child, you are obsessive aren't you? What does it matter to you about Gloria?'

I bit my lip. 'I'm just asking.'

'If you really want to know, she's a nightmare. She smells of beer and she's terribly rough. She scrapes the skin on my back when she hooks me up. I believe she does it quite deliberately.'

'Then why don't you get rid of her?'

She sighed, again. It was beginning to get on my nerves.

'I could come back and work for you, if you like. I'm not busy at the moment.'

She looked at me with her most sombre expression. 'My darling, it's out of my hands. I told you, my life is not mine any more. I am owned, like a chattel, by the management. It's terrible. They dictate what I do and who I hire and virtually what I eat.'

'But if they want you so badly they'd want you to be happy, surely.' She didn't reply. 'It makes no sense,' I went on, and then when she didn't respond to this I blurted out, 'I don't believe you!'

She swivelled in her chair so she was facing me directly. 'Now listen, darling, you have no idea. What do you know about the theatre? You were with me for, how long – a couple of weeks?'

'Nearly a year.' An exaggeration, but not a huge one.

She looked genuinely surprised. 'Is that right? Well, that was then, when I was a struggling artiste. I am now . . .' She paused, as if searching for the right word. 'I am, for my sins, a successful actress. I have sold my soul.' She clutched her bosom, which looked to me as if it still firmly belonged to her, as did her soul, if she had one. 'It's what happens when one achieves success. One is no longer in control of one's life, one is subject to the whims of other people – one's employers and one's public. One has obligations one never had before, when one was young and carefree.' There were an awful lot of 'ones'. She'd become altogether rather pompous, and the helpless little woman act didn't sit naturally with her at all.

'But there is another thing.' She placed her hands on her lap and looked down at them. 'This is quite hard to say, Prudence.'

I don't think she'd ever called me Prudence in her life.

'The thing is . . .' She looked up, and at the corner of the room. 'In the time we were together, much as I appreciated your company and everything you did for me, you were marvellous in so many ways, I didn't feel our relationship was . . . entirely healthy. Do you know what I mean?'

I did not. I stared at her in astonishment.

'I can see you have no idea what I'm talking about. It's called infatuation, darling. We've all done it, it's part of the business of growing up, one has little sense of proportion. In your case I felt it was, shall we say, *excessive*. So I thought it best to put a stop to it. Hence Josephine. I knew she wasn't the right person from the start but I had to . . .'

'Get rid of me.'

'Not like that, darling. I did it for your own sake.' She put her head on one side again. I couldn't stand being looked at sideways, it was like being patronised by a parrot.

'Why didn't you say something?' I almost shouted.

'Well . . .' She raised her eyebrows. 'What was I supposed to say? I thought it might be kinder not to say anything, if you want to know. And now look at you, you're upset. There is really no need, you know. It's something we all go through, as I say. But it's not entirely healthy, not really.'

That was more than I could take.

It wasn't that she was telling me something that I knew to be true and didn't want to be told. There was an element of that, of course, but that I could take. It was her tone, the tilt of her head, the talking down, as if to a child. I was no longer that. I was twenty years old by then, a young woman, thank you very much – and only a few years younger than *you* I'd have you know.

None of this I voiced out loud, needless to say. I just sat there and bristled, while Stella laughed in an embarrassed sort of a way, then shook her head at me as if to say, 'What are we going to do with you?'

I made my excuses and got up to go, and she made no attempt to stop me.

So another chapter of my life closed its doors on me.

8

It was not long after my *contretemps* with Mrs Pat that I realised my father had lost his job.

The clue was his presence in the house in the daytime. I didn't give it much thought at first. In my self-centred naivety I assumed he had retired, or was on extended leave. It was the empty larder that gave the game away; that and my mother's apologetic smile when I complained, rather rudely and thoughtlessly on reflection, and she shrugged and muttered something about falling on hard times and having to tighten belts.

It was the only time I came close to regretting my upbringing. Liberating though it was, it had rendered me unemployable. Too uneducated to be a teacher, or even a governess; too clumsy to be a dressmaker or a bookbinder; too gentrified to work in a factory or in service; too squeamish to be a nurse and, worst of all, too ignorant to know how to go about finding work in the first place.

The only other possibilities were wife – not appealing – or concubine – more appealing in many ways, though demanding more passive dependence than I believed myself capable of.

I confided in Sacha. It didn't seem appropriate to spread the word too far and wide that I was so poor I was forced to go out to work for the first time in twenty years. He fortunately knew of a woman who owned a flower

46

shop and was in need of assistance. That lasted one day when the lady in question came to tot up at the end of it and discovered that her new assistant, though cheerful enough and an excellent saleswoman – she had never before had so many customers in one day – was incapable of calculating the correct change.

My brother, the accountant, who was by now living elsewhere with his wife and sending money regularly to help us out, said there might be a position at his company for a clerk. I said something to the effect that I'd rather sleep on the street, to which he responded to the effect that that was probably where I belonged, if the street would have me.

I spent a day in the public library leafing through a book called *A Dictionary of Employments Open to Women*. It added nothing to my knowledge. I scoured the advertisements in the newspapers, to no avail. I was caught in a complete bind: too well-bred for manual labour, too incompetent for anything else.

The one thing it did do, my predicament, was to focus my mind upon the notion of purpose and structure. You could even say it was the first time in my life I had had anything like the former, though not yet the latter. This confirmed my previous notion that real purpose can only be attained through hardship or need, a notion with which Sacha heartily agreed.

So my newfound purpose took me to Regent Street and there, in a small street off Savile Row, I found myself a position as a waitress in a very exclusive teashop. The manager was not in the least put out by my lack of experience; in fact he seemed to take quite a shine to me, or to what he called my cheerful demeanour and 'refined' manner with the customers. Refinement not being something I had ever been accused of before, I assumed he was really referring to my upper-middle-class background and posh speaking voice, which gave his establishment 'class' and made up – or so I assumed – for my inability to get an order right or handle money. The wages were laughable but the tips were excellent. I had a workmate called Sarah, a young lass from Yorkshire, who fortunately was a whizz at the till and whose Victoria sponges were second to none, but who became tongue-tied in front of the admittedly rather formidable lady customers. Which meant I was able to spend more and more time chatting and less and less time at the till. I gave Sarah most of my tips, which was only fair, even if it did rather negate the original point of the exercise.

I met some remarkable women, among them a seemingly mild-mannered but ferociously intelligent lady who introduced herself to me as Mrs Fawcett. One of the first things she asked me was why an educated person like myself was wasting my time waiting on tables, to which my response was, 'Needs must.' She frowned at this and asked to know more, and when I told her there really wasn't anything more to tell, that sounding posh didn't mean I was educated, she laughed and said, 'We will continue this conversation another time,' and left me a handsome tip (which I gave to Sarah).

I mentioned her to Sacha and he exclaimed, in awe, 'My word, Millicent Fawcett!' He went on to tell me that not only was her sister, Elizabeth Garrett Anderson, the first woman ever to qualify as a doctor, but that Mrs F herself was a writer and campaigner for women's rights and – 'Surely even you know this, Rudi!' – one of the founders of the suffragist movement.

Well, we all know now, in the heady 1920s, about the suffragettes, of Emmeline Pankhurst and her cronies. But back in the old '90s I was not the only one to have given no thought at all to what was popularly known as 'the plight of women'.

Mrs Fawcett took to me immediately. She described me as a perfect example of what disenfranchisement can do to a woman at the end of the nineteenth century. Forced to wait on tables because in lean times there was nothing else for me. I tried to protest it wasn't the fault of the politicians that I was too uneducated to be a teacher or too clumsy to sew dresses, but she wouldn't hear of it. She insisted I attend one of her meetings and attach myself to her 'cause'.

If ever there was a woman with a purpose it was Mrs Fawcett. She was not the only one. There were dozens of them, women mostly but not entirely, in all shapes and sizes, all united in the cause of Changing the Laws of Suffrage.

It was quite an eye-opener. I knew I'd had what most people would regard as a privileged background. I had parents, more or less, a home and enough to eat, as a general rule. That was not true of everyone, by any means. What's more, nobody had tried to tell me how I should behave or what ideas I ought to have. Up until that time I had always regarded my lack of education to be an advantage. I was what I considered to be a liberated woman, free to do and think as I liked.

But not the suffragists. To them I was 'repressed', along with the rest of my sex. Forced to marry, often unsuitably, for reasons of survival. Expected to live according to one's husband's whim, to hand over one's possessions and one's rights to him, to submit to all manner of mistreatment, with no redress, and in the case of breakdown of the marriage, compelled to hand over the children.

Put like that I could see their point, although their argument seemed to be more against the idea of marriage than the law. 'But it is the law!' they cried. 'It's the law that restricts the opportunities for a woman to earn her own living, to be independent, to think for herself! It is the law that pushes her to marry inappropriately!'

I had to grant them that, even though I had no intention at that stage of marrying anyone, inappropriately or otherwise. At the same time I could see no difference between my own predicament and that of someone like Sarah, who was infinitely more skilled than I was in the cooking department but didn't happen to have the gift of the gab – or more to the point, the right background – to be able to wheedle decent tips from the clientele. *That*, I tried to point out to them, was where the unfairness lay.

They insisted suffrage would put a stop to that, that even the likes of Sarah had to gain by having a say in how the country was governed. Putting aside their reference to 'the likes of Sarah' I struggled to see how she, or I, or pretty well any female I'd ever known, could begin to understand the workings of government *and* decide what would be best for one and all.

They nearly stoned me then. They called me 'the enemy within'. If women couldn't unite amongst themselves what hope was there for any of us?

Well. Now. I understood enough about politics, and about the vote, to know that power didn't rest entirely in the ample lap of our beloved Queen, or even in the hands of the Prime Minister, whoever he might be. I knew enough about parliament to know there were good men and true whose knowledge of the world was a great deal wider than mine, and whose job it was to create laws that they believed to be for the common good, on my behalf. I was perfectly happy to leave the whole tedious job up to them while I carried on with my own life, and if there was something they were doing that I disapproved of, well then I would make my thoughts known one way or another.

But what I was not prepared to do was to be dictated to

by a mob of strident women who thought they had the right to tell me how to think. This was not something any man had ever dared do in the whole of my life, I told them, and woe betide anyone who tried.

Well, you could have dropped a pin. I think I even frightened myself. Their faces were a panorama of astonishment and disbelief.

It was Mrs Fawcett herself who broke the silence. She came up to me, kissed me on both cheeks and announced to the world in general, 'My dear Prudence, you are just the sort of woman this movement is looking for!'

Thus began my career with the suffragists.

9

Things moved rapidly after that. I gave in my notice at the teashop, with some regret as I'd become rather fond of it, and in particular of poor Sarah, whose face was such a picture of distress when I said goodbye even I shed a tear or two. And I aligned myself with the fearsome women suffragists.

If I was looking for purpose I had found it. There was enough of it among the suffragists to go round the entire population, female and male. There was even structure, after a fashion. One was supposed to put in regular hours and the days got longer as time went on. The work was not necessarily interesting; it was mostly posting leaflets and arranging meetings and standing around outside parliament on freezing winter mornings hoping to lobby MPs.

Some of the fearsome ladies had been at it for years, and between you and me it didn't seem we were getting very far. To have purpose to no end must be the height of purposelessness, but my fellow workers disagreed, with vehemence. Purpose is nothing without persistence, I was told.

The meetings took place in different suffragists' houses, most of them in Kensington and terribly grand. At times when they carried on into the early hours, which was often – how those ladies could talk – I was invited to stay the night. This is how I came to make the acquaintance of a lady called Violet Magenta Rose Turnip. Yes, her actual name, she told me with a shriek of laughter. Given to her for the most part by her batty mother, but the ridiculous vegetable tagged onto the end the result of her marriage.

Mr Turnip did not, fortunately, look like his name. On the contrary he was an exceptionally handsome man, and aware of it, and travelled everywhere with a cane which he twirled like the ringmaster at a circus. He was fond of childish jokes and delighted to meet someone like me who appreciated them. We spent many merry hours over dinner laughing ourselves stupid.

Mr Turnip, Anthony, was naturally excluded from the meetings and what he made of them, or of his wife's preoccupations, I had no idea. The subject was never discussed between them, so far as I was aware. Which was odd in itself, though I didn't necessarily think so at the time.

It wasn't until I told Violet that really it was time I returned home for a while that she grabbed hold of my sleeve and said, 'Please Prue, don't go,' with such intensity I was quite taken aback.

'I really need my things,' I told her. I'd been wearing the same clothes for so long they were almost glued to my body. 'But I can come back if you like.'

I didn't need much persuading. In my absence from home my mother had turned my bedroom into what looked like a sewing room, with a treadle machine set up in one corner and various garments strewn over my bed. My dressing table was covered in cotton reels and ribbons and buttons and who knows what. When I expressed my surprise, having never seen my mother so much as thread a needle before, she said it was for 'pin money' as she put it. I asked her since when had she learned how to make dresses and she said, 'Oh no, I'm not making anything, I'm just patching up and darning.' And she looked almost apologetic.

I was surprised to find myself quite depressed, and guilty, that my mother, at the age of fifty-something, was having to take on such a lowly and badly paid task as repairing other people's clothes. And she at that stage in her life not at all well. I wondered if I should resume my job at the teashop and at least contribute something to the failing household expenses, and decided I would talk the whole thing over with Violet.

She greeted me on her doorstep with such effusiveness I forgot for the moment all about my guilty feelings. She sat me down and listened while I explained to her my mother's predicament and how I felt it was time I 'did my bit', which of course meant I could no longer work for the suffragists. She screwed up her face in dismay.

'If it's money that's the problem then we can help you!' she exclaimed. When I told her that was absolutely out of the question she cried, 'It's the least he can do!' Then she thrust a hand over her mouth and I noticed, as I hadn't before, that she wore a glove.

She was agitated in a way I'd never seen in her before. She fluttered her gloved hand in front of her face for a moment, at the same time as she tried to hide her other naked hand in the folds of her dress. I raised my eyebrows and without looking at me she murmured, 'Chilblains.' There followed a pause while I continued to stare at her and she continued to look around the room and at anything but me until we both burst out laughing.

'I think you'd better tell me everything,' I said, as gently as I could.

~

I have always been surprised, and almost impressed, by the extent to which a woman will go to remain loyal to her spouse.

In my world if a man beats a woman she should leave him. At the very least she should call the police. Failing that, she should tell her friends. Anything, *anything* rather than keep it to herself. I never saw the point of keeping anything to myself; in my view that's the first step on the road to martyrdom.

I had known Violet and her husband for some time now. I'd lived in their house and shared their meals and conversations. I had Anthony down as arrogant, but no more so than most men, possibly exaggerated by his extreme good looks, which never did any man any good and no woman either. What I took to be his indifference to Violet's absorption with the suffrage movement was no more or less than one might expect from a conventional man of the time.

What I didn't know, and never even suspected, was what went on in their bedroom late at night, after those long meetings when – let's face it – he had been completely ignored by his spouse and her female campaigning friends. My bedroom was on the floor above theirs but I never heard a thing. No shouts, no thumps, so the ferocious arguments that Violet told me about must have been conducted in near silence, which made the whole torrid business infinitely more chilling.

She began by removing her glove and showing me the scratches on her hand. They were livid, and slightly swollen, as if she'd had an argument with a cat. They'd been done by her nail scissors, she said, in response to her insistence that just because she didn't know the name of the Secretary of State for the Colonies did not mean she did not have the right to vote.

It seems her charming husband, following our marathon meetings, would quiz her in her bedroom on current affairs. He would start with asking her who was the Prime Minister and move on to the Home Secretary and the Secretary of State for Foreign Affairs. This was usually not a problem, Violet tittered. It was when he moved on to affairs of state, and in particular what had happened in parliament that very afternoon, some bill that had been passed, or maybe not passed, and the reasons why and what the ramifications might be – that's when she faltered. She tittered again. 'He told me if I spent less time talking nonsense with my lady friends and more time paying attention to what is actually happening in the world, I might consider myself worthy of the vote.'

We stared at one another blankly for a long moment.

'And of course he has a point,' she concluded.

I tried to tell her that not understanding the ins and outs of the latest Enclosure Act (she laughed at that) didn't mean a person was too ignorant to have a say in things. And nothing, but *nothing*, gave anyone the right to stab someone else with nail scissors. She laughed again at this and stuttered that it wasn't he who stabbed her.

'It was him or me,' she said simply. She wasn't smiling now. 'And I thought it would be safer to be me. I didn't think I had a violent bone in my body. I used to rescue wounded birds when I was a girl. I once brought a cat into the house that had been kicked by a horse and it died right there in the living room, in front of my mother and me.' She was weeping now. 'I would never, ever hurt anything or anyone. Never!'

That stopped me in my tracks. To think a woman like Violet, the gentlest person you could meet, and tiny – tinier than me even – with tiny features, and always a soft and welcoming smile on her face, could inflict violence on anyone, let alone herself, was too bizarre for words.

'So what are you going to do?' I asked her.

She looked down at her hand for a moment. 'It'll heal,' she said, replacing her glove. 'I'm told it's better if it's protected but not covered in bandages.'

'I meant about Anthony.'

'You won't say anything? You absolutely promise? I'm afraid it would ruin everything if you did.'

I promised not to. But I vowed to think of something.

That's what the suffragist movement was all about, I realised then if I hadn't before. How many of these women had husbands who bullied them, even beat them, and they hung on for the sake of the children, or the house, or for their future.

I learned more. I learned that Anthony blamed Violet for not producing children for him, as if it was her fault; and even if it was, how could she do anything about it? I saw how a victim of bullying like Violet suffered twice over, from the bullying itself and from the self-hatred that arose out of her acceptance of it. I began to see the whole suffrage movement in a new light.

~

I wasn't going to confront Anthony, not in front of her, I wasn't that stupid. Besides, there were not many moments we were together without Violet in the room. But that same evening when I arrived back on her doorstep – and by now she was wearing gloves on both hands as if it was the most natural thing in the world – she left the room to visit the lavatory and there was just him and me. He was reading the newspaper.

'So,' I said brightly. 'What do you think of the cause?'

'What's that?' He looked over the paper at me and scowled, then remembered I wasn't Violet and smiled.

'Women's suffrage. What do you think of it? What's the man's view?'

He laughed shortly. 'I don't give it much thought.'

I nodded. 'Too busy with what's going on in the world, I suppose. What *else* is going on in the world.'

He lowered the paper and seemed to contemplate for a moment.

'I have no objection if it keeps her busy and makes her happy.' And he resumed his newspaper.

'You don't hold out a lot of hope then? For success?'

'Not so long as they keep squabbling among themselves.'

'What do you mean?'

He lowered the paper again and folded it and laid it on his lap.

'Well, what is it you women want? It would help if one knew. It would help if the right hand knew what the left was doing, and maybe even agreed with it.' He laughed at his little jest. 'Some of you want the vote for married women, some of you for unmarried women' – he waved a hand in the air – 'some of you don't even want the vote at all. How can you have a say in the running of the country if you can't even agree about what it is you want?'

I let that one rest for a while.

'There is more than one party in parliament, isn't there?' I said. I wasn't terribly sure of my political facts, but I was pretty sure of that.

'What's that got to do with anything?'

'If everybody agreed with everything . . . if men agreed on everything . . . there would be no need for more than one party, would there? You wouldn't need an opposition. You could just sign away the bills – "Oh yes old boy of course, quite right, I quite agree, now how about a game of billiards?"'

He looked at me as if I was mad. 'What are you talking about?'

'I'm trying to say that since not all men agree on anything, is it so surprising that not all women agree as well? Isn't that what makes life interesting?'

He shrugged. 'Until women can present a clear idea of exactly what it is they want then there really isn't any point in the whole argument. There are other far more important matters going on in the world. It's best if they keep out of it.'

'"They"? And do you mind my asking why?'

'I'd have thought it obvious. If Violet is going to concern herself with outside matters, where will she find the time for the home? It does take some looking after, you know.'

'I'm sure it does.'

'If Violet were to go away and leave me in charge of domestic matters I wouldn't know where to begin.'

'That's a shame,' I said, as daintily as I could. 'But I'm sure you could learn.'

'I doubt it.'

'Why is that? Surely, if a woman can understand parliament, a man can understand the home. Or does it not work that way?' I carried on before he could interrupt. 'Is it because a man's brain after all is not bigger than a woman's?'

He looked at me in incomprehension. 'I'm sorry, I don't follow your argument at all.'

'Do you know how to make a woman climax?'

It came out rather suddenly and unexpectedly. He stared at me.

'To make a woman what?'

He was still staring at me when his wife re-entered the room.

Poor poor Violet, I thought, he doesn't even satisfy her in the bedroom.

10

Meanwhile I had not been neglecting my other duties. The hedonistic weekends in the country continued despite the fight for women's suffrage. Perhaps not surprisingly the topic never arose in conversation among the gay young things, and when I tried to introduce it I got nothing but blank stares.

Now I've never really been one for the countryside, all that nature and so forth. I've always found it frankly *dull* compared with the bright lights of London. But I did enjoy those country weekends, especially in the spring and summer when it was warm enough to sit outside in the fresh air, being decadent. And decadence in the fresh air sounds positively health-giving. Moreover there was always Something Going On.

An outsider, looking on, might see nothing more than a pleasant rural scene, like something out of Jane Austen, with women and men of varying degrees of beauty and elegance lounging by the little fountain and going for gentle walks through the formal gardens. I can picture us now, like a series of watercolours in some art gallery that Sacha used to drag me around on rainy afternoons in London.

But the insider knows different. The insider recognises these country scenes as microcosms of the world, where battles are fought and won and skirmishes break out in surprising places, and now and then something really shocking happens. None of this is evident to the outsider because among the terribly well-bred the surface is all calm, and smiles, and laughter, and now and again a little lighthearted playfulness that may be followed by a little lighthearted scolding. You'd think it was the Garden of Eden if you didn't know better.

It was on one of these idyllic days, in April if I remember correctly, when the hedgerows were bursting with blooms and the English countryside was looking, and smelling, at its absolute best. We were waiting for a big announcement. We had deliberately left the happy couple alone inside in the study of whatever grand house we were occupying at the time. Gerald, grumpy Gerald, was marching up and down on the lawn outside, taking the odd bad-tempered swipe at the grass with his croquet mallet. He was bad-tempered not just because the croquet had been delayed, or more likely cancelled altogether, but because of what he, and the rest of us, knew was going on inside the house.

It was a scene of suspended animation. The attention of all was on the window of the study, through which we could just about make out two heads, together in conversation. Those of us who were close enough could see those two heads come together in a kiss, and there was a communal drawing in of breath as we struggled not to clap our hands together in congratulation. Any moment now there was to be an announcement: the final coming together, the engagement, of the two most beautiful and loved members of our little community.

Time passed. Only minutes actually, though it seemed like an hour. The two heads vanished into the shadow away from the study window. Conversation resumed, albeit in a desultory way.

Then Dougie emerged through the side door of the

house, on his own, looking rather wan. Nobody paid him obvious notice, but our eyes were on the door behind him as we waited for Claudia to emerge, all smiles; even though anyone who knew Dougie could guess from his expression that all was not well.

But he smiled, rubbed his hands together and looked from one to another of us as if to say, 'So, what's up? What games are we going to play this afternoon?'

Soon afterwards Claudia appeared, smiling shyly in her customary way. She walked in an unnecessarily large circle around Dougie, who rather deliberately did not look at her. She came straight over to me, tucked her arm into mine and marched me off towards the formal gardens, hissing as we went, 'What are they all staring at?'

'What do you think?' I hissed back.

'Just because Dougie and I . . .' She didn't finish.

'Yes?'

'Oh God, Prue, do you think I've made a terrible mistake?'

'I've no idea. It would help if you told me what went on in there.'

She shook her head. She was marching us so fast I was almost tripping over myself. We'd reached the far end of the rose garden and as we turned to go back we were confronted by Gerald, of all people. He was standing right in our path, his croquet mallet slung over a shoulder.

'There you are,' he pronounced.

To my surprise, and partly to my horror, I saw Claudia give him a beaming smile.

'Ready for another game?' He was addressing Claudia, of course.

'Yes, why not?' she said, and releasing herself from me she transferred her arm and her attention to Gerald and they walked away from me without a backward glance.

I didn't get another chance to talk to Claudia that day.

She went out of her way to avoid me, and when we did eventually bump into one another the following morning and I said to her, 'You were saying?' she looked at me nonplussed for a moment before smiling ruefully, studying the ground and then shrugging. The nearest she got to confiding in me was a vague, 'Well, it didn't work out, did it?'

Dougie didn't appear to be particularly put out, though I did catch him once staring moodily into space, which was not like Dougie at all. And so life went on as if nothing had happened, until the evening of the final day of the long weekend when Gerald and Claudia announced their engagement to be married.

You could have heard a pin drop. For one wonderful and ghastly moment those bright young things let down their guard completely and stared at both parties in outright astonishment. And in the long silence that followed I distinctly heard Dougie snigger.

I took him to bed that night, and held him while he sobbed. You would have to know Dougie to appreciate how extraordinary that was, that a man who was the life and soul of wit and fun and everything that makes a community like ours worth wasting time on, was capable of such searing, profound emotion. He kept on telling me he couldn't understand it – Gerald, of all people – and I stroked him and agreed with him and tried not to tell him she would come to her senses, she would change her mind, he just had to hang on. Because I didn't somehow think she would. I had no idea what went on in Claudia's head that weekend and I still don't.

We made love fervidly, as if it was our last night on earth. He reached into me like a lost man, spilling into me all his despair and his grief. I held him as tightly as I could for as long as I could until I felt his rigid body relax, and then I stayed awake all night listening to his snores.

11

I could have fallen in love with Dougie at that moment but it would have been a disaster. Besides, I didn't think I was capable of falling in love with anyone, not after I'd witnessed the agony he went through. I couldn't ever imagine finding myself so wracked with grief about anything or anyone.

There is something shocking about seeing someone who is normally so in command of himself in a state of raw grief. It exposed Dougie to me in ways in which his naked body, and the intimacy of that night, could not. I could say it bound me to him for life, as a friend you understand, and I suspect he felt the same.

The whole incident proved to me that Claudia was, after all, the cold fish I had taken her for from the start. How could she have led Dougie such a dance, encouraged not just him but all of us to think that they were made for one another, whilst knowing all along that she was in love with Gerald?

In love with Gerald, God help us. Grumpy Gerald. Graceless Gerald. They were not just my words for him. The one person who seemed to understand was Sacha. He compared Gerald to Dougie as a rope to a piece of thread: the tough to the fragile, the constant to the transient. I laughed at him. I think I even accused him of being a bit in love with Dougie himself. He just inclined his head and said, 'She made the right choice.' But he was the only one who thought it – apart from Gerald, of course.

I told Claudia I wanted to take her away for a few days, a kind of last-chance fling before she tied herself to that oaf forever, somewhere like the South of France. Her eyes lit up – 'Oh, wonderful idea!' – and they didn't even flicker when I told her I had no money so we would have to be inventive.

We wound up in Cap Ferrat, which was on the sleepy side, perhaps a little too much for my liking though it seemed to suit Claudia. We sat on deck chairs in the sun and drank cocktails and it was decadent beyond belief. I had a little fling with one of the waiters, which Claudia thought was too outrageous for words; but somehow she didn't disapprove, in fact I think she quite envied me for my lack of inhibition, not to mention taste. There was a ridiculously handsome and obviously filthy rich Frenchman staying in the hotel who couldn't take his eyes off Claudia. 'Go on,' I said to her, 'he's yours for the picking. One last fling before you enter purdah.' He bought us drinks and tried to follow us all over the place, which activity I positively encouraged, though it wasn't very kind of me because Claudia was simply not interested at all.

I used to watch her at times when she didn't know it. I marvelled at how she could remain so consistently elegant, even when asleep, how she kept her mouth from dropping open and dribbling like the rest of us mortals. Was she truly a goddess? If so, could Gerald handle her? Could anyone?

At last we got to talk about Dougie.

I did not, needless to say, tell Claudia he and I had spent the night together; but I did tell her of his extraordinary feelings for her. She arched her eyebrows at me and said, 'Oh?' *So you've been discussing me behind my back*, was the implication.

'I sensed it,' I said, rather lamely. 'And frankly you could see it in his face after you turned him down. The word is "devastated".'

She laughed and said she didn't think Dougie was capable of deep emotion, that he was one of life's charmers and there was really very little to him that didn't meet the eye. He was a flirt, incapable of taking anything seriously, really not marriage material at all. I knew she knew she was spouting nonsense from the way she rattled on, not looking me in the eye, her voice getting louder and louder as she tried to convince herself as well as me that she hadn't made a monumental mistake.

'But why Gerald?'

Of all people.

Because he was solid. That was the actual word she used. Solid, reliable, steady and terribly clever. One of the leaders in the field of archaeology, known throughout the world and so on. Awfully interesting. Never short of conversation. 'I will never be bored,' she concluded.

As reasons for marriage go, that wasn't a bad one, I admit. But it wasn't the whole story.

I didn't like to think how he might be as a lover. Somehow the vision of Gerald making love to a woman made me want to laugh. Poor Claudia. On the other hand she was such a virgin – and by that I don't mean to say she had never been deflowered, though I'm pretty sure she hadn't – but I struggled to think of her losing herself with a man, in bed or anywhere else. I couldn't imagine the goddess letting her hair down, or allowing herself to be seen naked, to be ravished, to cry out with pleasure and passion – all the things I had done with Dougie (and a few others). I had a horrible feeling Claudia wasn't too keen on sex in the first place, not that we discussed it, not then. She wouldn't.

Poor Gerald, I thought.

I've never been one for close friendships with other women, truth be told. I don't include Stella of course – that was something else.

Or maybe it wasn't. Maybe there were similarities between them, Stella and Claudia, or at least in the way I viewed them. They were both in their different ways unreachable. They were both goddesses.

Claudia was a terribly difficult person to read and that's partly what made her attractive to me, and it was very much the reason I suggested our sojourn in the South of France in the first place. I wasn't quite sure she was real. I wanted to poke her, figuratively speaking, to see if she'd react. I even thought I might learn something from her, pick up a bit of her *sang froid*, stop to think before opening my mouth, to be *appropriate*. Claudia was always appropriate. I'm not ashamed to admit I wanted to be a little bit like her.

It wasn't that I thought I could change her mind about marrying Gerald. Crikey, who did I think I was? If anything, I hoped I might get to the root of what went on in her head. I couldn't forget her plaintive – 'Oh God, Prue, do you think I've made a terrible mistake?'

So I watched her with the terribly handsome and rich Frenchman, whose name was Bertrand, it transpired. The more he ogled her that evening the cooler she became, until I swear she drifted off onto another planet altogether right in the middle of the conversation. I could see Bertrand was bemused, and bewildered, as being French and rich and handsome, and very obviously married, he considered it his duty to seduce any beautiful woman he came across. I don't imagine he'd ever been thwarted before. Claudia's indifference puzzled him, but the more she withdrew the more he persisted, and the more he persisted . . . and so on.

It was a wonderful game to watch. There are many times I've been grateful for my own plainness as it gives me the opportunity to watch the beautiful ones at play. They are not like the rest of us, they don't have to work for everything as we do, they can just sit there in their loveliness and let the world come to them. I could see Bertrand had never had to try so hard before and didn't quite know how to go about it, yet he didn't have the wit to let it go. There is a difference between playing hard to get and being genuinely indifferent and he couldn't spot it.

I began to feel quite sorry for him. And slightly guilty for having egged him on in the first place. In the end Claudia got to her feet and announced that she was starving and ready for dinner, and with a brief nod to Bertrand she wafted off up the steps towards the hotel. I watched her go for a moment and then I leant over and gave the poor man's hand a squeeze as if to say, 'Oh well, *c'est la vie* and so on, there are plenty of other fish in the sea, one of which is right here with you by the way, hmm?' But he didn't seem to see me.

This episode threw a new light on Claudia, and I began to realise what made her tick and why she had chosen Gerald over Dougie. Of all the men I'd ever seen her with Gerald was the only one who didn't spoon over her. Perverse, maybe, and hard for the likes of me to understand. But that's what it's like for the beautiful people, it all comes too easy to them, and as we all know, if it's easy then it can't be worth much.

Hallelujah, I say once again. Who would want to be beautiful?

~

The wedding was marvellous, of course, and Claudia was beautiful and looked, I admit it, perfectly happy. Dougie smirked his way through the ceremony and whispered nasty things into my ear about Gerald's morning suit. It's true that Gerald did look uncomfortable and kept shifting about as if the lining of his jacket was making him itch. He mumbled his 'I dos' and was obviously hugely relieved when the whole thing was over. He genuinely didn't like being the centre of attention and retired to the sidelines at the first opportunity, leaving Claudia to the admiring limelight of our friends.

After that I lost touch with Claudia for a while. She spent much of her time overseas with Gerald on whatever dig he was working on. And then there were babies, one after another at regular intervals, which understandably took up most of her time and attention, and since I'm not one to go gooey-eyed over the little squalling things we pretty well lost touch.

Besides, I had my suffragists.

12

'What did you say to him?' asked Violet. It was the morning following my brief tête-a-tête with her husband, approximately one second after the front door had closed on him.

'What?'

'Last evening, when I was out of the room.' She took a little bite of her toast.

'I can't remember. Oh yes. I asked him his opinion on the suffragist movement, and he said what was the point of it when we couldn't even agree on anything amongst ourselves? I said isn't that why there's an opposition party in parliament, because men didn't always agree on anything? That's all.'

Violet dabbed at her mouth with her napkin.

'And I may have made a comment about the size of men's . . . brains.'

'Ah.'

'Why?'

She placed her napkin carefully upon her lap, then she arched an eyebrow and said, 'Well, I'm terribly afraid he doesn't want you under his roof any more.'

No surprise there. But I did my best to look surprised, and disappointed.

'It's never a good idea to get one over on Anthony.' She pulled a face. 'I could protest of course – I did protest as a

70

matter of fact. But all we'd be left with is a complete grump who'd do all he could to make both our lives a misery. Still, you can congratulate yourself on a pyrrhic victory.'

A pyrrhic victory, whatever that meant. I could guess. A victory that was not a victory, that left all parties in the same place they were in before. Or in my case rather worse off. But I didn't regret a thing.

When you thought about who should have the vote and who should not . . . When you thought of those vacuous young men whose fathers happened to own a little corner of Sussex because their fathers had owned it before them and theirs before them, set alongside the Violets of this world, who'd taught themselves Greek and knew everything there was to know about the classical world, there was no sense in it at all. And no matter how many leaflets you stuffed into how many envelopes, it wasn't going to make a blind bit of difference. What we needed was direct action.

Action rather than words.

The suffragist movement had been in existence for around fifty years by then and had got precisely nowhere. I soon learned why. The party who were most sympathetic to the cause, the Liberal Party, wouldn't vote for female suffrage because they thought women would only go and vote for the opposition, the Tories. It was stalemate.

Up until then the ladies had conducted themselves with the utmost decorum, and strictly within the law. It was years before the Pankhursts stormed onto the scene with their ideas of civil disobedience, so in that respect I was well ahead of the times.

I said to my sisters in protest, 'We must up the stakes, raise our voices and turn ourselves into headline news. Tell the world all about us!' And if that involved the tiniest bit of law-breaking, and even going to prison and becoming martyrs – wasn't that what Parnell and the Irish were doing, for not dissimilar reasons? I had learned that from Sacha. 'They can ignore what we say but they can't ignore what we do.'

Mrs Fawcett looked horrified. Even Violet balked at the idea of doing anything as vulgar as heckling at meetings or stamping on the feet of policemen outside parliament. That was the whole problem – they were all too darned well bred.

I didn't plan anything. It was while we were standing outside the House of Commons, my sisters in protest and me, trying to keep out of everyone's way, politely waiting for the powers that be to emerge so we could ever so respectfully collar them, that I decided enough was enough. I walked up to the entrance of the building and before anyone could stop me I marched right on through into the lobby, grabbed a chair, clambered onto it and began to shout. I can't remember exactly what I said, but it was something like 'We women demand the vote! Action not words! We are not going to be ignored any longer! Votes for women!' It was seconds before the police arrived and pulled me down from my perch, with a great deal of roughness I'll have you know, and manhandled me out of the building, past the little group of well-bred sisters, their mouths agape, and off to the nearest police station.

I was looking forward to my first experience of prison. I could see the newspaper headlines now: *Society Lady Locked Up! Protesting Woman Storms Parliament!* They couldn't ignore a thing like that. I'd be the heroine of the protest movement.

They kept me waiting for three hours. Then a tired-looking policeman sat me down at a table and asked me some routine questions: who I was, where I lived, could I read and write, had I been in trouble with the law before and was I loyal to our beloved Queen, and did I realise that by entering without permission into the seat of government I was breaking one of the most sacred laws of the land?

'Yes,' I said.

He hesitated for a brief second, before continuing. Did I realise that punishment for such a gross misdemeanour could involve me in a prison sentence, or worse?

'Yes,' I said.

He then went on at some length about the law and how societies could only remain civilised if they retained due respect for it, which to any civilised person should be blindingly obvious, even to a female. That it was all the more surprising that a woman of my obvious background, with the privilege of education and respectable parentage, should find herself the propagator of an act that threatened the safety of an entire nation. And that should other women of a lower rank be encouraged to follow my example the country as a whole would in no time find itself in a state of complete anarchy, thus undermining centuries of civilisation, tradition and heritage and the very fundamental principles of democracy.

That seemed a little rich, so I said nothing. But I felt proud to think that my little act of defiance had threatened the safety of an entire nation. *Trespass Threatens Democracy!* screamed the headlines. *Single Woman Brings Down Government!*

The policeman leaned back in his chair eventually, took a deep breath and said, 'Very well Miss Brooks, you may go home now.'

'What?' I stared at him.

'You will be escorted by one of my colleagues. And you will remain within the four walls of your house for twenty-one days.'

'You mean you're not locking me up?'

'We have neither the space nor the necessary

workforce,' he said wearily. 'Just don't do it again. Because if you do, there will be consequences.' He looked at me as a parent to a recalcitrant child. 'Do you understand me, Miss Brooks?'

'Don't you want to know why I did it?'

'I know why you did it,' he said, with some irritation. 'You made that blindingly clear.'

'Well, at least I got the message across,' I said. I went on sitting there.

'And if you want my opinion,' he continued, 'if women think they can walk into parliament and shout slogans, that's reason enough not to give them the vote in the first place.'

'You don't get it, do you?' I said.

'Oh, I think I do.'

'We've been going on about this for years and you didn't listen. If you'd listened, we wouldn't have had to do this in the first place.'

'We?' He perked up a bit at that. 'You mean there were others?'

'There may well be,' I said. 'In the future. Your prisons will be full of them. Of us. You'll have your work cut out then, I can tell you, so you'd better do some recruiting now if you don't think you've got the necessary workforce. This isn't just an isolated incident, you know, we're going to be manning the barricades. Or should that be womanning,' I laughed, but he didn't join in, 'until you sit up and take notice. *Votes for women!*'

I was desperate to get inside that prison cell and he knew it. He also saw a madwoman sitting opposite him who he had no intention of keeping under his roof for a second longer than was absolutely necessary. So he called for his colleague and bade me goodbye saying, 'And I hope we don't meet again, Miss Brooks.' And there I was, outside on the street.

I walked home, from Westminster to Clerkenwell, with this pipsqueak of a policeman who looked as if he should have still been at school marching along beside me, occasionally grabbing hold of my sleeve as we crossed the road – to make sure I didn't make a run for it, I imagine.

My mother's face on the doorstep was a picture.

'What's happened?'

'She got herself into a bit of trouble,' said the pipsqueak. 'She's to stay inside the house for twenty-one days.'

'What kind of trouble?'

'Just a silly prank,' he said, with a smirk. 'Nothing too serious. But keep an eye on her, would you, Mrs Brooks?'

'How do you know my name?' Her eyes widened.

'It's all part of the job,' he winked. I badly wanted to kick him, and very nearly did, except my mother pulled me through the door before I could get at him.

~

And that's how I came to be living at home again.

To avoid my mother's questioning look I immediately went upstairs to my bedroom, remembering too late that it was no longer my bedroom but a sewing factory. The bed was now covered in scraps of material, dumped on top and in the middle of the clothes that presumably were there to be mended. It was a good thing their owners couldn't see the chaos. I did a rough job of sorting one from the other and piled everything on top of my dressing table and any other piece of furniture I could find, then I lay down on the bed.

A few minutes later there was a tap on the door and my mother appeared. She came over to the bed and sat down next to me, looked at me rather nervously and said, 'I am so sorry.'

'What for?'

'For being such a bad mother.'

'What?'

She looked away from me. She was awfully thin, I noticed, and quite drawn, either because she was unwell or even, I thought with horror, because she wasn't getting enough to eat.

'What do you mean, for being a bad mother?'

'A policeman!' It had obviously frightened her quite badly, seeing her daughter turning up on the doorstep with a man of the law. In her book policemen were people you asked directions of when you were lost, which in my mother's case was most of the time. They also, I realise now, would have reminded her of my childhood, when after a day's fun and games on the streets a man in blue would happen by and, realising I was truanting, as they put it, would march me home to confront my mother on her doorstep with, 'Is this yours?'

'It's all right Mother,' I told her now, 'As he said, it was just a silly prank. They'd have kept me in if they thought I was a real risk to society.' I spoke through gritted teeth.

I didn't think there was much point in trying to explain everything to her. But I was concerned, and really quite moved, that she thought it was somehow her fault. If ever I had children, which was extremely unlikely, I would consider anything they did as soon as they were old enough to do it without me, to be their responsibility. I was, after all, a fully-grown adult.

'I don't really know anything about you, do I?' She wrinkled her nose anxiously. 'I never know where you are, or what you're doing.' She frowned, and then she thought of something. 'Are you married?'

'Dearest Mother,' I leaned back into my pillow. 'If I ever get married you will be one of the first to know.'

She nodded. She was twisting a handkerchief in her hands which were, I noticed, skin and bone and so riddled with arthritis all the joints were in the wrong place.

'You don't look at all well, Mama,' I said, and reached over to take one of them. It was cold and bony and so tiny it disappeared completely in mine.

'No,' she said vaguely. 'I feel rather tired all the time.'

I played with her hand. 'How's the mending business going?'

'Oh, not too badly.'

'Looks like you've got plenty of work.'

'Yes, I'm a bit behind. My hands aren't what they used to be, you see.'

'You haven't been a bad mother, Mama.' I stroked the knuckles on her hand and gently pulled on one of her fingers and she flinched. How she could even thread a needle with hands like those, let alone mend socks, was beyond anyone's imagining.

'I had the best upbringing.' I placed her hand back on her lap. 'I really did. You didn't tell me what was right or wrong, I found out for myself, and that's the way it should be. It did me no harm at all.'

'But look at you!' She was staring at me in some distress. 'Look what's happened to you!'

'What do you mean?' I sat up on my elbows. I wasn't having that.

'Not married, at – at – how old are you now?' She didn't wait for an answer. 'And coming home on the doorstep with a policeman?' She was becoming quite agitated. 'I didn't know anything about having children, what was I supposed to do? Nobody tells you! Nobody tells you what you're supposed to do! And now it's come to this . . .!' She snatched up the poor mangled handkerchief and blew her nose.

'It's come to what? Mama, what are you talking about?'

'We've always . . . we've always . . .' she was pulling at her nose with the handkerchief so hard I thought it might come off in her hand.

'Stop doing that!' I grabbed hold of her hand so hard she let out a little yelp of pain. 'I haven't been up to anything. If you really want to know, I was breaking the law because it was necessary, because it's almost the end of the century and it's high time – *and* we have a queen as head of state, which makes even less sense – it's high time we women were given proper recognition!'

She was staring at me.

'Recognition for what?'

'For being women! We want representation and responsibility and allowed to be fully-grown human beings with brains and opinions and voices, and . . . and . . . The right to be considered equal to men.'

'Equal to men?' Her eyes had grown very big.

'Yes. What's wrong with that?'

Poor woman. It wasn't what I'd intended. In fact it was precisely what I was trying to avoid.

She was gazing at me as if I was speaking in tongues.

'Equal to men.' I could see her mind ticking over, watching herself going out to work with her briefcase and umbrella – she always was rather literal-minded, my mother – while my father washed up the breakfast things. The image of it made me laugh suddenly. She looked at me sharply.

'I was just imagining Father doing the washing-up,' I explained.

'And cooking the dinner.' Her little pinched face puckered with merriment. 'Doing the laundry, and the shopping – oh my!' Her hand flew to her mouth as she let out a gale of laughter. 'Oh dear me, Prudence. Can you imagine?' she almost whispered, and we held onto one another and laughed ourselves silly for a whole minute.

Of course I couldn't leave her to it, not after that. Certainly not with all that detritus littering my bedroom. I told her if I was confined to barracks for three weeks I would at least try to be a bit useful, even if it was a case of the blind leading the blind. How difficult could it be to sew a hem or mend a sock?

I won't pretend it was enjoyable. It was hard work, and not particularly satisfying, though it got easier the more we did it, and the better at it I became. We began to turn it into little games. We'd make up stories about the owners of the socks, who used to belong to the exclusive men's outfitters Toffs & Swells in Jermyn Street, or the owner of the evening gown that had been patched and mended so many times there was very little of the original garment left. Mr T & S and Mrs Not-So-Grand used to frequent the Savoy every Friday evening and dance the foxtrot, and it was oh so romantic and they knew all the names of the waiters by heart and everyone was always *so* pleased to see them so they got the *best* table and the *fastest* service. And now that they've fallen on hard times and can't afford the Savoy any more they recreate the scene of their courtship in their living room, dancing around the room to an imaginary orchestra and waving at their imaginary fellow guests, before taking their seats at their dinner table and smiling at imaginary waiters. Meanwhile their actual neighbours watch them through the undrawn curtains of their window in wonder and disbelief.

It was all terribly stupid, but terrific fun. And the twenty-one days slipped by very quickly.

13

One day Sacha burst onto the scene again.

I was now twenty-two and I hadn't seen Sacha for years. Nobody in the family seemed to know where he was or what he was doing, and when I mentioned his name they couldn't wait to change the subject.

I was annoyed with him and told him so. I could be dead for all he knew, or cared. 'Oh but you aren't, you are alive and looking exceptionally well,' he said, 'as I knew you would be as you, darling Prue, are a survivor.' When I asked him what he meant by that he said I was the sort of person who could withstand life's strings and arrows (that's what it sounded like) unscathed. That I had a unique ability to weave my way through the fog of life to find the one sunny corner in a murky world.

Fascinating to see yourself as others see you.

He told me he had indeed quarrelled with his family when he quit law school. He'd somehow made his way to Berlin and had fallen in with a group of artists and poets and acrobats; all of whom were terribly well bred but starving because, like him, they had turned their backs on conventional society and their families' expectations and had chosen the life of the poor yet liberated artist. 'Because there is nothing,' Sacha declared with some passion, '*nothing* more valuable than one's freedom.'

He felt he had come home. Here, he said, were the

80

soulmates he'd been looking for his whole life, and while he spoke virtually no German he was able to communicate perfectly. They all lived in one big house, many people to a room, some of them sleeping on the floor, with no heating and sometimes very little to eat. Yet he never felt hungry, or cold.

I personally could not see the attraction, let alone the point, of starving for your art, or for anything else for that matter. However I could see Sacha had found his own version of purpose. He did look a bit scrawny, he'd lost a good deal of weight and his complexion was quite pallid, but his eyes were as bright as ever. He'd fallen in love, of course, many times over, mostly with men but on the odd occasion with women too. I told him he was promiscuous and he laughed loudly and said, 'Hoorah!'

I asked him how he'd made a living and he said he'd tried his hand at being an acrobat. He'd become quite proficient on the trapeze, and he told me what a thrill it was every night, knowing that a split-second's mistake could mean the difference between life and death. That ended after a falling-out with his acrobatic partner, who happened also to be his sexual partner, after which Sacha felt, understandably, that the split-second mistake might happen at any time.

So he'd turned himself into an artists' agent. He'd noticed that while his superhumanly creative housemates were able to churn out masterpiece after masterpiece, sometimes several in one day, they weren't so creative when it came to doing anything with them. So the canvases piled up against the walls, apparently forgotten, until you could hardly move for them. When he asked his friends what they intended doing with the paintings they shrugged and said it wasn't their business, they'd done their bit and it was up to someone else to deal with them. That miraculous 'someone else' presumably being some rich patron who would arrive, telepathically, on their doorstep happy to exchange their masterpieces for wads of cash. Even Sacha thought that was naïve, not to say downright lazy.

He sympathised, of course. When it comes to selling their work every creative person has to brave the real world of commerce, which most creative people consider beneath them. So he took it upon himself to do the sordid commercial bit for them, touring the galleries selling their paintings and pottery and suchlike, which, though he said it himself, he turned out to be really good at.

What got to him in the end was the lack of gratitude, or even acknowledgement, on the part of his housemates. They didn't seem to notice that their works of art had been miraculously transformed into food, and alcohol, or if they did they thought it was no less than they deserved. That, Sacha explained finally, was what did it for him. It all ended in a monumental row.

'I sold five paintings today, Eric,' he told his Belgian friend. Eric had been one of his earliest lovers and was, in Sacha's view, the most talented of them all.

When Eric didn't respond Sacha repeated himself, and added, 'I managed to get a good price for them, we have enough to eat now for at least a month or more.'

Still Eric said nothing.

'Are you hearing what I'm saying?'

Eric finally looked at Sacha through hooded eyes. 'So?' he said. 'It is no more than they are worth. What did you get for them? They were worth at least five thousand each.'

'Five thousand *each*?'

'You mean you sold them for less?' He made a 'pouf!' sound and carried on painting.

'Do you know . . .' Sacha snatched his friend's paintbrush right out of his hand, 'what it takes to sell a painting in this beleaguered city? Do you know how many streets I've had to trudge down, how many doors I've had to talk my way through?'

Eric shrugged.

'And that's just the beginning. Then I have to stand there while some Philistine – because believe me, there are plenty of Philistines in Berlin, especially in the art world – looks your painting up and down with what I can only call complete indifference, while I regale him with some fanciful explanation as to what the painting is meant to represent, making it up as I go along for the most part because you – *you* – refused to tell me. Do you have any idea how many times I have had to talk my way into a sale because otherwise no one in those galleries would give me house room?'

Eric shrugged again and said, 'A painting is not a kitchen implement. It does not need to be explained.'

'That's all very well for you to say, you haven't had to go out there and convince someone the untidy mess I am showing them is actually a post-modern representation of present-day urban paranoia, part of the Bla-bla movement which in no time is going to take the art world by storm and is worth five thousand marks.'

'What are you talking about?'

'I'm talking about the kind of gibberish I have to invent to convince people to buy your fucking paintings!' Sacha flinched. 'Forgive the language, Rudi.'

'Did you really say that?' I laughed.

'These artists think they are so precious.'

Sacha went on to say that many of these artists' movements, so-called, were actually made up by people just like him, on the spur of the moment, for the sole purpose of impressing owners of art galleries who wouldn't know a Michelangelo from a dog turd.

I said I would give anything to spend a few days with

Sacha in his furniture-less mansion, preferably in summer. He told me on the contrary I wouldn't, I really wouldn't. And besides, he had quite burnt his boats with his friends in Berlin, and was now trying to infiltrate what he said was the fledgling London version of the Berlin set, which he thought was based somewhere in Bloomsbury. And once he'd done that, he would be knocking on my door again and introducing me to the likes of the writer Virginia Stephen and her sister Vanessa, who was a painter. I tried to look impressed and failed. Dear Sacha.

14

The end of the century came and went, and I celebrated its passing in what Sacha described as a 'dive' in the *banlieues* of Paris with a middle-aged French *gentilhomme* with more money than sense, which was what I needed to do at the time. I eventually returned to London and drifted from job to job. I spent several months looking after the spoiled and neglected children of a widowed businessman in Knightsbridge, a challenge to say the least. We had a lot in common, the precious little ones and I, when it came to our experience of childhood abandonment. But whereas I had just about managed to pass myself off as a human being, these two creatures had turned into little savages. I would take them on daily walks to Hyde Park, as instructed, and as often as not I came home without them – they having run off through the trees and refused to come when called, like untrained dogs. The little dearlings always managed to find their way home again, sometimes in company with a policeman but more usually on their own, and looking almost sheepish, I was pleased to notice. I acted as if nothing was wrong, nobody was concerned with their whereabouts, so their attempts at drawing attention to themselves fell flat.

The master of the house thought I was miraculous and for one awful moment I thought he might be on the point of proposing. So by way of diversion I told him if he continued to ignore his own children he could hardly blame them if they did outrageous things in order to get his attention. That was the end of that position, and not a moment too soon.

Then I obtained employment reading to an elderly woman with failing sight. She was sweet-natured, and soft around the edges, and she smelt of rosemary and pine. We began with a hefty tome called *Middlemarch,* and at Sacha's suggestion moved on to Thomas Hardy. That's to say, that is what she thought I was reading. She liked the sound of my voice, she found it soothing, and truth to tell ten minutes in and she was snoozing away in her armchair, snoring gently. So long as she could hear my voice she could doze for hours, but the moment I stopped she was wide awake. After a while I gave up on the books – I found Thomas Hardy almost more tedious than George Eliot – and told her real stories, about myself and people I knew; about Sacha and his Berlin acrobats, and all sorts of exotic nonsense, most of it true. I realised much later she had heard every word, but she didn't want to interrupt because, like me, she found my stories so much more compelling than Mr Hardy's.

Towards the end of January 1901 the Queen died and was replaced by her son Edward – popularly known as 'Bertie' on account of his first name being Albert. Why he couldn't have been King Albert rather than King Edward VII is beyond me. Luckily and by contrast with his gloomy mama, Bertie was a merry soul with an unconventional private life. The world suddenly came alive as a result. At around the same time my father found a new position, which meant my poor mother could at last turn her back on having to mend other people's clothes, and I could take a break from working in unspeakable jobs for unspeakable people and get back to the important business of enjoying myself.

They were strange times. The merry, philandering King set the tone with his households of mistresses, and in society at least, it seemed anything went. I had a few dalliances – a Bulgarian prince (so he claimed) with money but no sense of humour. A Turkish croupier with no money but a great sense of fun.

I then became embroiled with the son of the Earl of Hampshire, the Hon Cedric Cockmeister (not his real name, of course). We met at one of those dinner parties I was constantly being invited to, as the still-single girl, in order to make up the numbers and pair off with the still-single bachelor. The Hon was not, needless to say, that same unattached single man. His wife was a beautiful but bored-looking thing who hardly spoke a word all evening. If she noticed her dearest paying more attention to most of the other women than he paid to her, she didn't seem to mind, or to care.

The Hon Cedric set me up in a *pied à terre* in Bayswater of all places. I had never thought of myself as mistress material; I was hardly an adornment on any man's arm, and I was, let's face it, heading for thirty. Moreover I was single, in an age when most toffs preferred their mistresses to be married, for a variety of reasons.

Before you pass judgement, may I remind you that the tone had been firmly set by the Prince of Wales, now the King. It was quite the thing for a married man of a certain class to have at least one mistress. Put rather basically, it showed to the world he had enough money to keep at least two women, if not more. Put even more crudely, it implied he had the sexual prowess of a stallion and the allure of a god. As for me, I did it for the fun as much as anything, in bed and out of it. Besides, how else was I going to get to hobnob with the aristocracy? It ended, as it had to, when he caught me throwing late-night parties he was not invited to. I was supposed to be at his beck and call at a moment's notice, but weeks would go by without a beck or a call, so what else was a single woman in her prime and all alone in her tiny nest in west London supposed to do of an evening?

The role of mistress was ultimately not for me, unfortunately. I had thought it meant comfortable living without responsibility, and I rather enjoyed the raised eyebrows and whispers behind fans at social events – there was never any real attempt to hide these things. What did it for me was the man's assumption that his mistress was his property and his alone; and while it was perfectly all right for a man, married or single, to take a lover or two, it was *not* all right for his mistress to do the same.

Someone suggested I follow in the footsteps of the famous Lillie Langtry and take to the stage. I gave it serious thought. I even tried to get in touch with Stella again – I've never been one to hold a grudge. She had become what they call an actor-manager, which meant, I concluded, that she was in a position to hire and fire as she pleased. She was working mostly in America then, but I managed to meet up with her in a teashop off Shaftesbury Avenue on one of her brief visits to London. She looked me over in her usual studied way and said if I cared to be her assistant she might consider it. I told her I was too old and too stupid to be anyone's assistant, so that was the end of that.

Meanwhile on a more serious level, the suffragists were beginning to sharpen themselves up under the beady eye of the formidable Emmeline Pankhurst. They even stole my slogan (more or less): 'Deeds not words!' Not to mention my call to civil disobedience. I contemplated joining the movement again but between you and me I felt I'd done all that could be done in that respect; and now other people had moved in and stolen my thunder I might as well let them get on with it.

There wasn't, as Sacha would say, a lot of point to anything I did around that time. My life was still gloriously purposeless. The difference was at my age it was all beginning to pall, the fun and games. I was approaching thirty. I was starting to feel old.

15

To make one thing quite clear: I have nothing against the institution of marriage. It is what I used to call 'a necessary evil', especially for a young or not so young woman in the early part of the twentieth century. The problem is I have seen too many friends marry for the wrong reasons – for money, for security or simply to avoid spinsterhood and escape the family home. Or worse still, for passionate love, that burns itself out in no time at all or drives the other half to distraction. All these reasons – or excuses, as I think of them – are entirely understandable.

The successful marriages, which include my brother's, only succeed because the wife seems perfectly happy to be dictated to by the husband. I am not drawing judgement on them you understand, I am stating a fact as I see it.

I'm sure there are strong women out there who are happily married, some of my suffragist sisters among them, presumably because between them, husband and wife have reached a kind of accommodation. A power sharing, so to speak. But one way or another it seems to me the odds against a happy marriage are stacked high.

I could never see myself as married, for a number of reasons, the most important of which was what Sacha called my over-developed resistance to boredom. I am easily bored, I admit it. None of my affairs lasted more than a few months. I never thought I could find a partner who could amuse me equally well with conversation and entertainment, sexual and otherwise, and keep it all going for the rest of my life.

Now some people have had the gall to suggest I have a low opinion of myself. True, I have come out with the odd stupid remark such as, 'Who would want to spend the rest of their life with me?' when anyone queried my single status. But that's just a way of putting a stop to a conversation when I know what they're really thinking is, 'Poor you, pushing thirty and still a spinster.' The truth is I know myself well enough to recognise I am impossible to live with. I am selfish, and self-willed, and I have a total resistance to anyone who tries to tell me what to do. That's in case you hadn't already noticed.

Then there was Dougie. You may remember we spent one passionate night together, and as lovers go, he was one of the best. There was a potential there that we were never able to exploit, mostly because all the time he was making love to me he was really making love to someone else. And no matter which way you look at it that is not a satisfactory state of affairs.

I've made love to foreign princes, English toffs and Cockney stagehands. I've made love in palaces and luxury hotels, in kitchens, behind the scene dock in a theatre, and on one memorable occasion in the back seat of a tram. I have lost count of the lovers I have enjoyed and couldn't begin to remember all their names; which is a shame because I would like to take this opportunity to thank them all and to tell them how much utter joy and pleasure they brought to me. If you are one of them and you are reading this, you know who you are.

Fond memories.

~

One night, quite late, I was arriving back in London by train after visiting friends in the country, and I was making my way along the platform when my right foot got caught in something and I couldn't move. The heel of my shoe, I saw, was stuck fast in the grill of a drain on platform 5 at Paddington station, and struggle as I might, I could not get it free.

'Can I help you?' He was tall and lanky and wore glasses and a suit and looked highly amused.

'I can manage, thank you.'

'Here, lean on me,' he offered. So I did, while I removed my foot from the shoe and, standing on one leg like a stork, bent down and tried to retrieve the shoe. The more I tugged and wiggled it this way and that, the more it refused to budge so the more flustered and embarrassed I became, all the time clinging on to the stranger's arm.

In the end I managed to wrench it free but the heel was no longer fully attached to the shoe. I replaced the shoe on my foot and, thanking the stranger rather cursorily, I hobbled off down the platform, aware that he was still watching me with that same amused smile. This made me quicken my pace until I stumbled and almost snapped my ankle in two. He caught up with me at the end of the platform and said, 'Are you hurt?' to which I muttered, 'Not at all,' which he could see wasn't true as I was wincing despite myself.

'Let me get you a cab,' he said, and grabbing my arm to steady me he marched me over to the cab rank, and before I had time to open my mouth he'd bundled me into the vehicle and told the driver to take us to the nearest hospital.

I protested, obviously. I said it was nothing more than a strain. But he said one shouldn't take a chance on these things and besides, there was St Mary's just down the road.

There was a fair time to wait to be seen, so we sat together, this stranger and I, in the antiseptic and decidedly unromantic surrounds of the waiting room at St Mary's Hospital, and told each other the story of our lives.

He began by telling me he was a secret agent. Or more to the point, a double agent. He had been recruited on a London street by a foreign power – he didn't say which one – and at their suggestion he had infiltrated a group of anarchists who met regularly to discuss ways of overthrowing the government. Among them was a failed scientist called the Professor, who liked to boast that he travelled about London wearing a flask containing explosives attached to the lining of his coat.

Unfortunately the anarchists seemed more interested in talking about overthrowing the government than doing anything about it, and the foreign power meanwhile was running out of patience. So they called my new friend in to see them and ordered him to prove his worth by blowing up Greenwich Observatory, adding that if he did not do as he was told the consequences could be lethal.

He gave this notion some serious thought, needless to say, and decided to ask the advice of the Professor. The Professor naturally jumped at the idea and promised he would deal with the business right away, and before my companion could stop him he'd jumped on a train to Greenwich and raced up the hill to the Observatory, but on the way he appeared to trip and before you could say cloud cuckoo land, he had blown himself up not fifty yards away from Greenwich Observatory.

Fortunately, the Professor was the only casualty. There then followed a sequence of complicated events involving various members of the police and the Home Secretary, during which the activities of the foreign power were exposed. So my companion was now in the throes of arranging an elaborate funeral at the expense of the foreign power for his late colleague – who, he made a point of declaring, had proved by this final gesture that he was not the failed scientist everyone had taken him to be and was, in fact, a loyal subject of His Majesty and a martyr to the cause of freedom.

In return I told my companion I was the widow of the King of Bohemia and that I had thirteen illegitimate children, all of them the offspring of royalty. I had a palace in Rome, a house in the South of France and a flat in London, with a dozen servants in each, and between them my children stood to inherit the throne of virtually every country in Europe.

It was the best I could come up with at the time. My new friend, who had not yet introduced himself, told me that for the mother of thirteen I was indeed in remarkable shape and that widowhood appeared to suit me.

I was quite sorry when I was eventually called to have my ankle attended to. As I suspected, it was only a mild sprain, but my friend insisted on hiring another cab to take me home and on accompanying me all the way. Before he helped me out of the cab he handed me his card, saying that if I had no objection he would call on me in the next few days to see how I was getting along.

His name, I was sorry to see from his card, was Wilfred de Vere. I told him there was no way in the world I was going to call anyone Wilfred, so he said as a special favour I was permitted to address him as Fred.

Fred kept his word. He was on the doorstep the next day, and the day after that and so on. We sat and chatted and for the life of me I can't think what we chatted about, except that it was always easy and fun and interesting. I found myself waking up of a morning and counting the hours until the ring on the doorbell, which usually came around 6pm as he was on his way home from work, he said. On fine evenings and weekends we went for walks in the park, which is not an activity I would normally have indulged in, but somehow Fred had the knack of turning the most tedious pursuit into something that was fun, and unexpected.

He was hugely observant – an occupational hazard for a spy, he maintained – and he had the craziest imagination. He'd make up stories about the old woman on the park bench for instance, who lived alone with five cats and a ferret who fought one another tooth and nail all day, so the only respite she had was these few moments alone on a park bench. Or about the strange man with the shabby overcoat who was actually a duke in disguise, forced to pawn his clothes in order to pay the rent on smart apartments in fashionable areas of London for his various mistresses; mistresses being, he told me with some authority, demanding creatures who expected the earth. I did not have the heart to contradict him, let alone confess I had once been one.

The one thing we rarely did was socialise. I wasn't sure Fred had any friends and he certainly showed little interest in meeting mine. Surprisingly this didn't bother me in the least, because I was only too happy in his company, doing silly things mostly, and laughing.

We got married six months later. It turned out his story was not entirely fantasy, even if the gist of it was taken from a book by Joseph Conrad.[1] He did indeed work for the Secret Service Bureau and he had been recruited on a London street, though not by a foreign power with the purpose of blowing up Greenwich Observatory but by a member of the Foreign Office who happened to know he spoke fluent German.

I was almost disappointed. I had fallen in love with Fred's imagination, so to discover that his story wasn't entirely fantasy was a bit of a let-down. Still, there was plenty more about him to enjoy. His wry sense of humour,

---

[1] *The Secret Agent*

his dapper appearance – he had the sexiest moustache, and I speak as someone with an aversion to the things – and above all his boundless imagination.

Who'd have thought it?

16

'Prudence Brooks is getting married.' You could almost hear the disbelief on friends' lips. 'Does he know what he's taking on?'

Nobody said that to my face of course, but I couldn't blame anyone for thinking it. After all, I was thinking much the same myself.

When I examine my reasons for getting married . . . Well, let's confess it, I didn't examine them, not at the time. But with hindsight, having reached the ripe old age of thirty-something and tiring of the endless affairs, I was ready for something new. Fred was not the most handsome man I had ever met, not by a long chalk, he wasn't even the most exciting lover, but he was very good company and above all he made me laugh. You will have recognised, if you've been paying the slightest attention to these memoirs, that that is number one on my list of priorities.

And yes, he was comfortably off. Not that that played a part in my decision-making, you understand, although a woman of my lack of talents would have been very foolish to have set up home with a pauper, certainly not back in 1911. I had no intention of settling down, mind. What a horrid expression. 'It's time you got married and *settled down*,' as if that's pretty much the end of everything. It's the sort of thing a mother would say. Not my mother, of course.

So there was to be a wedding, and I was to make it a big one, a day nobody was going to forget. I was going to invite everyone: my silly friends from our gay country weekends, and Dougie, who didn't respond, to my consternation – someone thought he might be living abroad – plus Claudia and her dull husband Gerald and their daughters. And my serious friends from the suffragists, including Violet and her vile husband. Then there was the immediate family of course, which meant Sacha, naturally, and Stella.

I hesitated over Stella, not because I didn't think she would come, but because famous people have a habit of stealing one's thunder even if they don't intend to, and I wanted to keep my thunder to myself.

I wore purple satin, just to remind people I wasn't intending to *settle down*. Fred laughed out loud, right there in the church, to the consternation of the vicar, so I knew we were stepping off on the right foot. Stella did come, on her own, and sat right at the back of the church, and it wasn't until some time into the day that anyone knew who she was. Claudia was there with daughters but *sans* husband, thank the Lord. Walking back down the nave of the church with my brand new husband was like seeing a panorama of my whole life spread out in front of me, pretty well everyone I'd ever known. Just like it must be before a bus hits you, Fred said later.

I don't remember much of the rest of the day. I do vaguely recall a party in a hotel, and champagne, and songs and celebration and more champagne, and Claudia's three daughters staring at me as if they'd never seen anything like it in their lives before. Oh, and Claudia reminding me that one of them was my goddaughter.

'Really, darling? Do tell me, which one?'

'Gracious, Prue, you mean you can't even remember?'

'It was some time ago, you know.' Well, around ten years since the middle daughter Harriet was born. I was glad it was Harriet, she looked like my kind of person, dead straight jet-black hair and dark, suspicious eyes. There was a lot to Harriet I thought, more than her sunnier-looking sisters. I apologised for being the worst godmother in the world – for isn't the godmother meant to be one's spiritual guardian? – and told her I hoped she'd been a good girl, and she just scowled at me.

Stella greeted me with a 'Look at you, Toffeehead!' and gave me one of her famous bear hugs. Then she did her thing of holding me at arms' length and gazing at me, and breathing, over and over, 'Look at you, just look at you,' as if I was something from another planet.

Stella inevitably did start nibbling away at my thunder but by then I was too far gone to care very much. She told wonderful theatrical anecdotes like the time she was playing Ophelia in *Hamlet* and Ellen Terry was in the audience, so she wore her real hair for the first act and donned a fair wig for the second, to impress the great lady, and nobody even noticed. I couldn't quite grasp the significance of this, not to mention the point, though I appreciated the fact that Stella was able to tell jokes against herself, which was something. Fortunately, Fred was able to fill me in on what happened later in the evening after the bride had a bit of a turn and had to be gently led upstairs to bed by her brand new husband, protesting, 'But it's my party, I'm not ready to leave yet!'

It was a happy day.

I don't remember much of the night, ashamed as I am to admit it. I was rather too far gone. But there were other wonderful nights, and many glorious days.

~

It may surprise you to know, dear reader (it surprised me), that I took to married life more than I had ever thought possible. Fred was not in the least put out by my total ignorance of world affairs, quite the opposite. The last thing he wanted to do after a long day's work was talk about serious things. He did not like to discuss his day much. Besides, he said he was bound by something called the Official Secrets Act, which I thought sounded outlandishly glamorous. I could never imagine my Fred, with his skinny frame and those funny little short-sighted eyes twinkling away behind his glasses, as a spy. He insisted he was not a spy, but you know how it is, the more a person denies a thing the more you know it's true.

We attended state occasions such as the coronation of King George V, an interminable affair that went on for so long – a whole seven hours – I thought I was going to faint with hunger, right there in Westminster Abbey. We watched the suffragists marching through London and I couldn't help but notice a distinct group of them picked out by silver badges, granted in honour of their prison sentences. I was irked to see they had succeeded where I had failed, but the movement had moved up a notch or two since my day. I had been, as I said before and Fred proudly confirmed, ahead of my time. Now they were chucking stones through windows and even burning buildings. A while ago I might have been tempted back, it looked like fun. But the attraction of a prison cell had vanished, now there was Fred. For the first time in my life I realised I had something to lose. It was frightening. Love makes you cautious. It even made me think I might be *settling down*.

Children never arrived, for some reason, which is probably just as well as I'd have made a terrible mother. Fred was resigned, but always hopeful. 'Shall we have another go?' he would say as we made our way to the bedroom at the end of the day.

'Oh yes, do let's.'

But I did have a goddaughter, and it was Fred's suggestion I invite her to stay, *in loco parentis*, whatever that means – like a mad parent, according to Fred. They travelled up to London together, Claudia and the three little Claudias, and we gave them lunch and had such fun and I said how I wished she didn't have to live in the deepest depths of the countryside. She laughed at that and said Wiltshire was hardly the depths of the countryside, but promised to come and spend some more time with us.

Harriet seemed perfectly happy to be left behind once they'd gone. She wandered through the house at will, gazing with those dark broody eyes into the corners of the rooms, fingering the ornaments on the mantelpiece and staring at the pictures with intensity. She announced she was going to be a sculptress when she was grown up, which naturally I thought was simply marvellous. I asked her if she knew anything about sculpting and she said of course she didn't, she was only a child, and then she turned to me with a look of guilt and apologised. 'I can't help my mouth,' she said. I told her she was a girl after my own heart.

I took Harriet and Fred to the theatre to see Stella. She was performing in yet another melodrama with a forgettable name, though however absurd the play somehow she always managed to weave her magic into it. Harriet was transfixed, and announced the moment the curtain had fallen that she had changed her mind and was going to become an actress. So we went backstage and I introduced her to Mrs Pat. I told her my goddaughter had been so inspired by her she was going to follow in her footsteps, at which Stella fixed her great eyes on Harriet and said, 'Is this true?'

Harriet stood her ground, brave girl. 'I may, or I may not,' she said, twirling her left foot.

'There is no "may" in the theatre, dear. There is only

"will". Where there is "may" there is doubt. And doubt, dear child, has no place in the theatre.'

Harriet continued to twirl her foot and stare back at Mrs Pat.

'All right then, maybe I will.'

Even Mrs Pat smiled at that. 'I like a girl with wit,' she said. 'But look here, child.' She swivelled so she was facing Harriet directly, and pronounced, 'I have one thing to say to you: "To thine own self be true".'

There was a dramatic pause. Harriet stared back at her.

'Shakespeare,' added Mrs Pat, with some reverence. 'In this world of theatre we spend all our time pretending to be someone else, so it's all the more important to remember who you really are.'

Then she turned her attention to Fred. She told him how delighted she was I had found someone to 'take me on', as she put it. 'She's not an easy girl,' she told him, in a stage whisper. 'I could tell you one or two things about her you need to know, but perhaps now is not the time.'

'I can always come back another day,' Fred stage-whispered back. 'When we're alone without – you know.' He jerked his head towards us.

What silly nonsense. But it was good to see Stella again.

17

Harriet was silent all the way home, which was unusual for her. When Fred retired to his study to do some work I asked her if she would like to join me in a snifter.

'What's a snifter?'

'A tot, a nip, a wee drink. I have Cointreau or Cognac.'

'Alcohol, you mean?'

'I won't tell your mama.' A fine godmother I was turning out to be.

'All right, just a tiny bit.'

I poured her a thimbleful of brandy. She sniffed at it, then sipped it, then pulled a face, exactly as I thought she would.

'It tastes a bit like medicine.'

'You've never tasted Cognac before?'

She shook her head.

'So, dearest goddaughter, what's on your mind?' She frowned and looked down at her glass, which she held on her lap. 'Anything you say will go no further than these four walls,' I added.

She gave a sigh and pulled at her lip, before replying: 'I don't know who I am, Auntie Prudence.'

'I'm not your auntie,' I told her. 'And even if I were I wouldn't want to be called one. Prudence suits me just fine.'

'Prudence.' She nodded.

'You are ten years old, darling girl, of course you don't know who you are.'

'I'm thirteen.'

'Are you really?'

'But how can you – what was it – "To yourself be true"?'

'You can only be true to the person you are at that particular moment,' I said. I was thinking as I was speaking. 'I'm not sure I know who I am either. In fact I'm not sure if that isn't what life is about, in the long run, finding out who your true self is. It changes. It goes on changing all through your life. You think you want something passionately one day and the next you find it doesn't really matter at all.' This was not like me, dispensing wisdom like this. But at least I thought I was fulfilling part of my godmotherly duty.

'Is that what happened to you?'

'It's what's happening now, even at my ripe old age. What Stella was trying to tell you – Mrs Pat – is that it's important to do and to be the person you are at any one moment; to do what *you* want to do, think what *you* genuinely think, not what you presume other people want to hear, or in order to be smart or clever or to impress people. Terribly difficult, by the way, we all struggle with it.'

'Are you true to yourself?' She looked at me shyly.

'My word.' That floored me momentarily. 'For the most part, yes. You're not drinking your Cognac.'

'I don't really like it. I actually think . . .' She placed her glass on the table.

'You actually think it tastes like cough medicine. Say it, I won't be in the least offended. Even if it did cost £50 a bottle.'

'Did it?' Harriet's eyes widened.

'I've no idea darling, I'm just joking.'

I sat down opposite Harriet and took both her hands in mine. They were small and delicate, and reminded me in some ways of my mother's, without the arthritis of course. Like my mother at that moment the girl looked tiny and vulnerable and troubled.

'You mustn't take anything Mrs Pat says too seriously,' I told her. 'She's a bit of a drama queen. Not that she doesn't mean well.' I hesitated. 'That sounded patronising, I didn't intend it to. You see, normally I wouldn't have spoken that last bit out loud, but since we're having a little honesty session – let it all out.'

'I want to do something important with my life,' said Harriet.

'What do you call important?'

'Something that makes me . . . that makes the world . . .'

'Something that makes you feel special, or that makes the world a better place?'

She nodded vehemently. 'Yes, that. A better world. I would like to do something to make this a better world.'

Dear creature. I remember thinking that very same thing once, for about half an hour, but I couldn't come up with any ideas.

'You could become a suffragette.'

'What's a suffragette?'

My word, I thought, these girls lead sheltered lives.

'They're women who campaign for votes for women. You haven't heard of them?'

She shook her head.

'I was one once.'

She sat bolt upright. 'You were?'

'We were called suffragists then. That was in the polite days, when all we did was lobby parliament and write endless letters and circulate endless leaflets and it got us precisely nowhere.'

I told her of my little episode with the police, bursting into the House of Commons and trying to create havoc.

'I thought it was time to raise the stakes, you know, to stop being polite. So I earned myself a prison sentence and was headline news in the national newspapers.'

'Were you?' She was leaning so far forwards she was nearly toppling off her chair. 'Were you really, Auntie Prudence? Headline news?'

Goddammit, what was I saying? I started to laugh.

'What's so funny? It must have been awful. Mama never told me this.'

'That's because . . .' I was struggling to stop laughing . . . 'it never really happened. Dear me.' I dabbed at my face with a handkerchief. 'Darling Harriet, that is a perfect example of what Mrs Pat was trying to warn you against.'

'Going to prison?'

'No, of wishful thinking, or trying to impress. Yes, it's true I did storm parliament and I did shout slogans but unfortunately it wasn't deemed dreadful enough to earn me a prison sentence, or a story in the newspapers. I made that bit up.'

Poor girl was totally confused now. She tucked her hands underneath her and stared intensely at the carpet for a few moments, then she looked up and said, 'But the bit about you being a suffra . . . That was true?'

'Oh yes. I served the cause for a while.'

She was looking at me as if I was the Virgin Mary.

'I think you're marvellous, Aunt – Prudence.'

No hero worship, please.

'I'm not really marvellous at all, Harriet. I did it for all the wrong reasons. I just wanted to draw attention to myself. That is my weakness. I admit it, I've never been able to overcome it.'

'So you didn't really care about votes for women?'

'Yes, of course. Who wouldn't? But now look at me – I

didn't stay the course, you see. I got distracted. I got bored. I get bored easily, and that's not something I'm proud of.'

She was still gazing at me with adoring eyes. You know how it is, the more you try to persuade someone you are nothing more than an ordinary flawed human being the less they believe you. So I'm not just a goddess now, I'm humble with it.

'I want to live in London when I'm older. Can I come and see you lots and lots, Aunt – Prudence?'

'Darling, as far as I'm concerned you can come here as often as you like. We could have lots of fun together.' She was frowning now. I don't think fun was what she had in mind. 'If your mother has no objection, of course. I could show you around, introduce you to my suffragist friends. They could do with some young blood, I'm sure.'

'Mama wouldn't like to see me going to prison,' said Harriet. She pondered on this for a moment and then she said, 'I wish you were my mother.'

Oh dear oh dear. Well, of course, we all think similar things at some point in our lives, don't we?

'Dearest Harriet, I know you don't mean that. You know it too. You have the best mother a girl could have, don't ever forget it.' I meant it, but I was flattered too. How much easier it is to be the godmother than the real thing.

But wasn't I just the same with Stella? I remember to this day my embarrassment at hearing myself telling her she was glorious. Oh, those heady days of youth! After all isn't impulsiveness another word for honesty? Isn't maturity just another form of repression? Suppressing thoughts and feelings because they might be deemed 'inappropriate'? At least I'd had the advantage of finding this out for myself. Some people, Harriet and her sisters included I have no doubt, knowing what I did of Claudia, had had it drummed into them from birth. It was to Harriet's credit that she didn't let her conditioning hold her back. I would have liked to have said something to her to that effect but I thought it might sound disloyal, or critical of her upbringing, which wouldn't do at all.

All this introspection was unusual for me, and exhausting. I told Harriet it was past both our bedtimes and we would continue the conversation another time. As we said goodnight she gave me an enormous hug, and I confess it brought a tear to the corner of my eye.

~

I was dying to ask Harriet about her father. After all these years I had got no closer to understanding why someone as beautiful (if a little vain) and sweet-natured (if a little vague) as her mother should plump for someone as unprepossessing as her father. Especially when there was so much competition, so much dash and debonair among the rest of our country set.

Gerald was an archaeologist and worked for most of the time overseas in exotic parts. Now that might attract some women, to have a largely absentee husband, but not Claudia. Claudia was very much a wife and a mother, she was born to it in my view. But Gerald. He was very clever, I knew that, but no good with women, no good at all. Polite enough – held doors open and so forth – but hopeless at the small talk. Happy to chat about Important Things but unable or unwilling to banter; and our set was all about banter. He didn't understand the rules. Or if he did he ignored them.

I think Harriet may have taken after her father. Such a serious little soul, so determined to Do Something with her life – now *that* she did not inherit from her mother. Claudia was never one for Important Matters, she was a perfectly normal woman who seemed happy to take life as it comes, with no burning ambition to be the next Marie

Curie or Florence Nightingale. At least I imagined that to be the case. When it came to reading her mind Claudia had always been Miss Inscrutable. It must be tricky to have such a person as a mother, I think.

Harriet's burst of affection took me aback. In fact I'd go so far as to say it moved me quite deeply. The following day she was all smiles and laughter, and she insisted on holding my hand all the way to the railway station. But when it came to goodbyes she started to cry.

'Come and see me any time, darling. Any time at all.' I gave her an affectionate kiss on both cheeks and waved a cheery goodbye.

~

I am not a particularly emotional person. Neither am I one for hiding what feelings I do have. I often imagine the two go together, that it's the quiet people – Claudia is a good example – who feel things deeply. I am all surface, big displays of warmth and affection but actually, darling, it's all a show and I'd do the same if you were my closest chum or someone I've only just met. This has pluses and minuses. I admit I find it easy to make friends, people do seem to take to me quickly, immediately even, though I say it myself; they equally quickly go off me too. I've made as many enemies as friends. But I'm not usually one to inspire affection, I know this. I am good company, 'good value' at a dinner party, but I don't think anyone, other than dear Fred of course, would miss me much if they never saw me again.

Sacha once told me I was the most contented woman he had ever met. I asked him what he meant by 'contented'.

'You are content to be who you are,' he said.

That was a bit profound for me.

'Am I?' I said stupidly. 'So you can read my mind?'

'I never met a woman before who didn't in some way

109

want to be other than who she was.'

'I wouldn't mind being thinner. And prettier. I hate my hair. Will that do?'

'Trivial. You're making it up as you go along. These things don't really bother you, you don't brood about them.'

'I don't brood about anything. I am unable to brood.'

'That is precisely what I'm talking about.'

Well, I suppose he was right. I'd never thought of myself in those terms before. It seemed to me to be a waste of time, brooding. You are what you are.

"To thine own self be true," didn't mean a huge amount to me, because it would not occur to me to do otherwise.

I could try to be introspective. I could try to educate myself, to 'improve' myself. Now and then I've toyed with the notion of being able to join in a conversation about Shakespeare for instance, or Isaac Newton or any other of those clever people. But I could not hold a fact in my head. Nor have I ever had time for people who write things, it seems to me a poor substitute for doing. I may be inspired by Marie Stopes, or even Emmeline Pankhurst – who followed where I led, though she would never admit it – but I can admire without wanting to emulate.

So, as I mused to my beloved husband later on that evening, it was all the more odd, and amusing, that Harriet, who wanted to Do Something Important in her life should apparently hero worship someone who had never done anything with hers. He said it was because I was a shining example of someone who was 'true to her own self', which I thought was quite perceptive for a man. And besides, he added, I was totally unlike Harriet's mother and everyone loves people who are not like their parents.

He surprised me sometimes, did Fred.

~

As the years wore on Fred was not just working longer and longer hours, he was becoming more and more preoccupied with whatever it was that was keeping him at his work. I knew enough to realise when that happens to someone like Fred the news, whatever it is, is not good. There were times when he was away from home for days on end. I did wonder if there might be a fancy woman lurking in some dark corner somewhere. But no, not Fred. Not when, as people were beginning to speculate, there was war threatening.

18

Fred was away when war was declared in August 1914. I had no idea where he was or what he was doing. I had no idea why war had broken out in the first place. I understood there had been an assassination involving the Archduke of Austria and a Serbian assassin but I couldn't see what that had to do with us, or with any other country other than Serbia and Austria for that matter.

I went to the War Office to find news of Fred. They informed me politely that he was overseas, possibly in Belgium or even in Germany, on a mission of top secrecy. I told them I was his wife and I had a right to know where he was. I think I quite frightened them. They gave me the name of some obscure town that may have been in Outer Mongolia for all I knew, and I suspect they only did that to appease me. As for what he was doing there, even they claimed not to know.

I'd never been concerned before. Fred had always maintained the work he did, though Important, and of course Top Secret, was not dangerous. I believed him because I wanted to, but that was in the peace, and this was the war, which was a different matter altogether. I couldn't sleep for worry. I could barely eat. Then, I think to give me something to do and to get me off their backs, the War Office offered me a job.

I told them I couldn't type or add up and was generally

hopeless at making things or at anything clerical. They shrugged their shoulders at that and asked me what did I think of driving a motor car? I said that sounded just fine to me, and so they put me to work ferrying members of the War Office from one secret destination to another.

Well, of course I'd never driven a vehicle before, but they weren't to know that. Fortunately there was Denis, a fellow driver, who taught me the ropes.

'Dead easy,' he said, 'even for a woman.'

I ignored that.

'The hardest thing is getting her to start up. After that, just put your foot down on this pedal, not too hard mind, and off you go. And this pedal here . . .' he pronounced it ''ere', 'this is for stopping.'

'What's this handle for?'

'Them's your gears. Start off in low then push her through to high when you pick up speed. You'll soon get the hang of it. When you hear her complaining you know you need to change her up.'

He came with me the first few times until his wincing when I ground the gears, and his muttered "Jesus Christ" every time I hit the edge of the kerb got too much for both of us.

'You're on your Jack Jones now,' he said, exiting the vehicle so fast he almost tripped over himself.

And on my 'Jack Jones' – I was proud of the fact that I knew what this meant, thanks to my friend Mikey – I did pretty well. True, I bumped the kerb a few more times before I got the proper 'hang of it' but I never hit a pedestrian, or a dog – though there were some close shaves. I even earned a reputation as the fastest driver in the team, which gave me a certain cachet. Harriet would have been proud. As would Fred, had he known.

I worked five days on, two days off. It was on one of my free days that a black vehicle arrived at my door and out of it climbed an important-looking man in a black overcoat and top hat. I could see curtains twitching all the way down the street. I thought perhaps I was to be asked to perform an important function, to chauffeur a visiting dignitary, royalty even. But I soon saw from his expression this was unlikely.

Clutching his hat in his hand, looking so grave I was tempted to laugh, he invited me to sit down in my very own drawing room before he announced to me, with the greatest regret, that my husband had been killed on active duty.

My brain shut down completely. You can't imagine it unless it has happened to you, it is impossible to describe. My gentleman caller then suggested a cup of sweet tea and even had the enterprise to ring for Clara, the maid, and order one. She looked at us both wide-eyed and retreated in fright, and the hand that minutes later brought the tray and then poured the tea was shaking so much it was a minor miracle she didn't spill it all over my lap.

I noticed a little stain in the corner of the carpet. It's funny how you don't see these things. I made a mental note to point it out to Clara, not that there was much she could do about it and besides, if I hadn't noticed it before now, I could probably live with it a while longer. I looked around the room for anything else that might be requiring my attention, at which the gentleman caller said, very softly, 'Are you all right?'

Am I all right.

I don't think there's an answer to that. Fred is dead. Am I all right. My husband is dead.

'How did it happen?'

'He was leading his men from the front.'

That was arrant nonsense. My husband was not a soldier. Was he?

'What do you mean?'

I could see his mouth open and something come out of it but it didn't seem to be making any sense. I thought - He's got the wrong person.

'Are you sure you're talking to the right person?'

He looked bewildered for a moment and then he nodded and said, 'Mrs Wilfred De Vere?'

'That's me.'

Then I think he went on to explain how my husband had been on active duty in France, and that he was in charge of a platoon and had taken his men over the top: 'leading from the front' he kept repeating, as if that made it better. An act of extraordinary courage, a grenade exploded, killed outright and immediately, possible posthumous award for bravery, full pension, was there anyone I would like him to inform on my behalf?

'Mrs De Vere?'

None of it made any sense.

'My husband worked in Intelligence.'

He cleared his throat.

'Did you hear what I said? He was not a soldier. He never commanded a platoon. He was a spy.'

He said something I didn't catch.

'I beg your pardon?'

He repeated something about being behind enemy lines. That didn't make a lot of sense either.

'I don't understand what you're talking about!'

Poor man. It was not his day. He fingered his hat nervously, cleared his throat again. Started off on another lengthy explanation, at which I told him to go. Just go. 'Yes, I'll be all right. Yes, I am on my own but I will not do anything stupid. There's a stain at the edge of the carpet.'

He looked genuinely alarmed at this. He started backing towards the door.

'If you need anything . . .' He handed me a card, at arms' length. 'Anything at all. Just say the word. Be right here.'

Poor man.

Damn you Fred. Damn you damn you damn you.

~

You don't realise you have a life plan until something comes along to destroy it.

Ridiculous though it may sound, there being a war on, I never anticipated that Fred might be killed in it. Having never expected to find a husband in the first place I certainly did not expect to find one and then lose him. I absolutely could not make it make sense.

I went back to work the following day. They told me to go straight back home again but I said to them, 'What for?' I wanted to keep busy, and I did. I worked a twelve-hour day six and sometimes seven days a week, till I was so exhausted I could barely see the road. When I bounced over the corner of a pavement yet again, missing pedestrians by a hair's breadth, I was commanded to go home and not to come back until I was completely rested and recovered.

I arrived home to find a telegram from Claudia: *Come immediately and stay as long as you like.*

I didn't have the energy to resist.

~

Claudia and her family lived in the house her husband Gerald had been born and bred in, a pretty place in Wiltshire that sat in the midst of rather splendid grounds, with a formal garden and fountain and even its own wood.

I'm not keen on the countryside as a rule, as I may have already mentioned. It's too quiet for me. I've never found nature, rolling fields with cows and sheep in them, particularly peaceful. However it was springtime and everything looked young and vital and bursting with health – all the things I was not.

The girls being away it was just Claudia and me, and she sat with me quietly, not asking any questions, not doing anything much, which turned out to be just what I needed. We talked of inconsequential things, the girls mostly and, in general terms, of Gerald.

Gerald was helping with the war effort somewhere in North Africa, she said. An administrative job of some sort, not on the front line, thank God. She winced as she said this and I knew what was going through her mind. For once I did not want to discuss it: not Gerald, not Fred, not the war, not this damn war.

There were young men dying by the thousands, millions, people's sons, half-grown. And worse, young men missing, possibly forever, presumed – eventually – dead. It was no comfort at all to know we were all in it together.

I hadn't had a proper conversation with Claudia since what I called her pre-honeymoon, when we spent those few days together in the South of France before her wedding. Strange it is how marriage can come between friends.

I told Claudia something of my exploits with the suffragists, of my attempt at civil disobedience and my failure to win a prison sentence. She listened with that half-disbelieving, half-admiring look on her face which she tends to wear whenever I tell her anything. I also told her I'd been driving a car for the War Office as part of my contribution to the war. Though why any decent person should consider it necessary to contribute to something so vile and unnecessary was another matter.

'How did you learn to drive a car?' she asked.

'By doing it. I'm the fastest gun in the west, so they tell me. I'm the one they call for when they need someone taken from A to B urgently.'

'That's wonderful and brave of you. I'm afraid I am no

use to anyone.' She waved a languid hand across her face.

'Have you tried?'

'What could I possibly do?'

'Work in a factory. Do clerical work. There's plenty to do. Anything the men can do, we can do.'

Her brow furrowed. 'I haven't really looked. Oh dear me, I suppose I should. But there are the girls.'

'Find someone to look after them. Lulu could do it, couldn't she?'

'Who's Lulu?'

'Your maid.'

'Lily? Oh, I don't think so. Well. Yes, I'm sure she's capable but I'm not sure I would . . .' She tailed off.

'You could open up your house, make it available to the war displaced.'

'The war displaced? Who are they?'

'Wounded soldiers. People who've lost their families.'

'Lost their families? What do you mean?' She was looking more and more distressed.

'Orphaned children, there are plenty of them. And their mothers. There are some desperate people out there.' I was enjoying this. 'You might get some rough types but, well, if you want to do your bit.'

'Oh.' She took out a handkerchief and blew her nose. Her brow was so furrowed it quite distorted her face. 'Perhaps I should. Perhaps if I knew how to go about it. Perhaps you could tell me.'

'And perhaps,' I leaned over and patted her hand, 'you could just forget about it. If they want to requisition your house, that's another matter. Cross that bridge when you come to it.'

'Requisition my house? Oh dear.' She stared at her hands for a moment, and then, 'You are so brave. And so enterprising. You put me to shame.' She addressed this to the floor.

She looked deeply troubled. I got a lot of pleasure out of teasing Claudia, she was such an easy target.

'I don't want to say anything good about this bloody war, but it's a shot in the arm for women,' I said. 'They're finding out all sorts of things about themselves, what they're capable of. They say the women work twice as quickly and far more conscientiously than the men. The men don't like it, not at all. If they don't give us the vote after all this then my name is not Prudence De Vere.'

It was pronouncing the name that did it. I'd always found it a nuisance, before, to have to change my name. I felt I was renouncing my family and my roots. I had never before so naturally thought of myself as Prue De Vere, and just as I was getting used to it . . .

Then out it all came. My anger, my disbelief, my denial – why him, why my Fred? He wasn't even on active service, why should he have to die? Why should anyone have to die? What was the point of this bloody war? Where was it going to lead us, when was it going to end, how many millions of our men would have to be sacrificed before someone saw sense?

She reached out and embraced me. It was like being enveloped in a fragrant cloud, the softness of her skin, the delicate fragrance of her perfume, her arms enfolding me, rocking me back and forth like a tiny baby while I sobbed so hard I thought my eyes would fall right out of their sockets.

19

The following day, the girls came home. Claudia ushered them away from me for a private conversation as soon as they arrived, after which they stared at me in silence, as if I had some contagious disease. Poor them, they had no idea what to say to me.

Jessica, aged around twenty, was the first to broach the subject. 'Mama told us what happened and on behalf of my sisters and me I just want to say how very sorry we are,' she pronounced solemnly.

She was taken aback when I laughed, needless to say. I think my emotions were running a bit raw then, unfiltered. I took hold of her head in my hands and kissed her on the brow. 'Life goes on,' I said to her.

Isn't it strange what death does? Death, if you haven't known it, is the unexplored country where people speak an unknown language only understood by the bereaved. I tried to be jolly, to reassure the girls that there is life after death. 'And please, there is no need to look so mournful, I am not Queen Victoria.' But it's as I said before, the more you try to reassure, the less they believe you.

Even Harriet was strange with me. I thought perhaps they were thinking of their father, away overseas who knows where, afraid of it happening to him. This awful war. No one able to behave like normal human beings.

There came a point when I could stand it no longer.

Much as I loved all those women, Claudia and all three of her lovely girls, I didn't think it was fair to go on casting such a pall over their lives. What's more, the quiet of the countryside was making me restless, and life had to go on, I had to get back to work before they forgot all about me.

~

I confess I went a bit mad then.

The first was Denis, my War Office chum, the one who taught me how to drive a motor car.

'Orl right?' is how he greeted me when I arrived back at work. I'd been away three weeks.

He was the first person, thank God, not to mention Fred.

'Just about,' I said. 'Have you managed without me?'

He gave me a cock-eyed look. 'Can't speak for anyone else,' he said obscurely.

It was good to be back doing something. Now the war that was meant to last just a few months was into its second year it seemed horribly as if this was what normal life was to be like from now on. Everyone looking that much older, and more tired and anxious and grey about the gills. 'Will this war ever end?' I asked of no one and of everyone. They just stared at me. War was life.

There were emergency meetings, night after night. Denis and I were working into the small hours, so much so that as often as not we didn't go home. We'd curl up on armchairs or, if we were lucky, on the sofas of some dignitary who'd forgotten to lock the door to his office. One night there was only one sofa so Denis said he'd toss me for it.

'Heads,' I said as he tossed the coin, and then, 'Tails.'

He stood with one hand covering the coin on the back of the other hand. 'Which is it?'

'Either. Whatever you like.' I was tired. I didn't really care.

He looked briefly at the coin and then covered it with his hand again and smirked. 'It's both,' he said. 'We share.'

'We what?' I'd heard him all right.

He had this stupid grin on his face throughout. He peeled off his clothes and stood there, in the middle of the room, stark naked, hands on hips, proud as you like. I tried to look shocked, to be little Miss Prim, to live up to my name for once in my life, but you know what? I couldn't be bothered. I liked what I saw and he knew it.

We made love right there on the leather sofa in the office of the Private Secretary to the Minister for the Interior. Or the Colonies. I neither knew nor cared. It wasn't very comfortable but it was what I needed. We made love right through the night, goodness only knows how many times. 'You'll be the death of me,' he said, more than once, as he ploughed into me, over and over. 'You'll be the death of me.' Hardly the most romantic of lovers, but who needs romance in those circumstances.

They say people went crazy during the war, no one knowing who was going to survive from one day to the next, the most unlikely coupling happening in the most unlikely places. I can't quite use that as an excuse for my behaviour, but then I didn't think I needed an excuse. I wasn't accountable to anyone but myself. 'Look on, Fred,' I'd say silently. 'Look what you've made me do.'

There was a young lieutenant, somebody's *aide de camp* or whatever they call them. The war had terrified the life out of him, he'd seen things he had no right to have seen, not at his age, not at any age come to that. I saw him sitting in the anteroom shaking from head to foot. I didn't even know his name but I just took hold of him and held him and squeezed him till he was gasping for breath. The shock of such intimacy from a total stranger stopped the shaking for long enough for me to bundle him into the car and drive him back to my house and put him in my bed and ravage him throughout the night. He made love like a madman, which is what he was, and the following morning he was so exhausted I couldn't wake him, so I left him there in my bed – in Fred's and my bed – while I went back to work, and when I got back later that day he was gone.

There were others. Officers, under-officers, somebody's cousin, a Romanian captain and a French sub-lieutenant, I can't even remember their names or how I got to meet them all. They fell in and out of my bed at regular intervals – goodness only knows what the curtain-twitchers in my road made of it all. But we were all crazy then. It was a crazy time. It was a terrible time.

And then finally there was Armistice. On 11th November 1918, the war to end all wars was over. No more wars. We were at peace. We were safe.

And the peace drove us even crazier.

20

With the end of the war came the end of my job, and I wasn't sorry. While the plucky young men of Europe were battering the hell out of one another it was good to be occupied, and strange though it may sound, while I was in the thick of it I had no time to sit and contemplate the utter dreadfulness of the whole business.

I was not the only female to lose her job. All those plucky women who'd eagerly stepped forward to fill the gaps left by the men who went to war, working in munitions factories or nursing or tilling the land, all of them were out of a job, just like that. Worse, nobody seemed to appreciate them or thank them for what they had done. They were expected to go meekly home and carry on as they had done before, as if the war had never happened. And all those women who, like me, had discovered talents they never knew they had, and had grown in confidence because of them, were now expected just to go back to being dutiful housewives and mothers and daughters. It felt like stepping back several years in time. Strange though it may sound, with the end of the war came a massive anti-climax.

But we got the vote, after a fashion. Some of us, that is. And the men had the utter gall to announce to the women who'd sacrificed their health, their reputation and their sanity to fight for the vote:

'Well, it would have happened anyway, sooner or later.'

So, just as I was beginning to enjoy the rest, and the freedom, into my life once again came Sacha.

I had begun to think I'd never see him again. He seemed to have vanished off the face of the earth. My brother and sister-in-law had no idea where he was, nor did they seem to care. Then just as I was assuming the war had got him, there he was, on my doorstep one morning in the summer of 1919.

He was changed. He was thin as a twig, his glorious golden curls had been cropped close to his scalp and his complexion, that peaches and cream look, was positively rugged. He looked older, yet he was the same bright-eyed Sacha of old. I stared at him as if he was a ghost returned from the dead.

'Dearest Rudi!' He gave me a bear hug and walked right past me through my front door, into my living room and into an armchair before I could say, 'Well, fancy seeing you again.'

I stood there for some time, gazing down at him. Dear Sacha.

'So, you're not dead,' I told him.

'I'm certainly not. Why are you staring at me?'

I told him he looked different, changed, for the better and for the worse. Naturally, one had assumed, due to the total lack of news of him, that he had not survived the war.

He'd been called up in the middle of the war, he told me in some indignation. At forty he was just, *just* within the age range for military conscription. At first he'd laughed in their faces. 'Could you imagine a queer like me with a bayonet?' he'd said to them. When this failed to impress he told them he'd decided to become a conscientious objector. He said it as a joke, but no sooner was it said than he was lined up and processed, as he put it, like a slab of spam; sent before a tribunal and asked to account for himself, and then packaged off to work on the land, like a serf. The land! 'Could you imagine a queer like me with a hoe in his hand?' he exclaimed.

I said I couldn't see why not. I thought it might have done him some good, the change in his complexion told me as much. He laughed.

'Were you worried about me?' he asked eagerly.

I told him not in the least, I'd had far more important things to think about. And anyway I could ask him the very same question. I added that his family didn't seem to know where he was or what he was doing, and he responded that yes, well, that would be because they were no longer his family.

It turned out his father, who'd died the year before, had cut him out of his will on the grounds that he was a wastrel for not pursuing a career in the law and a coward for being a conscientious objector, and he deserved what he got, which was nothing. Sacha brushed it all off, claiming he couldn't care less. It was no more than he had expected, he said, he didn't want the old man's money and wouldn't have taken it anyway.

I told him that was outrageous, that he looked half-starved and in need of a hearty meal.

'I'm perfectly all right.' He gave me his brilliant smile. 'Top hole. Fit as a fiddle.'

'When did you last eat?'

'Why, only yesterday!'

He was such a child. I wanted to kick him, or kill him, if the starvation didn't get him first.

I took him out to dinner to feed him up. He ordered steak, rare, and demolished it in minutes. Then as he was forced to sit and wait and watch me picking at my poached trout he told me about his war.

It had been, as it turned out, rather remarkable. After a few months working on various farms in the Midlands, where he became quite a dab hand with the hoe, he'd been sent to work on a farm in Oxfordshire that belonged to a mansion called Garsington Manor, the home of Sir Philip and Lady Ottoline Morrell.

Here he paused, for some kind of effect. Clearly I was supposed to have some idea who he was talking about.

'And?' I said.

He sighed with exaggerated disappointment. The Morrells were a famed couple apparently, he for being a member of parliament, she as a society hostess and confidante of some of the most powerful men in the country, from the Prime Minister down.

He described to me the day he first set eyes on the utterly glorious Lady Otterly, as he called her. He was cleaning out the hen hutch at the time – 'my very *least* favourite job, Rudi' – when this 'vision' approached across the field and introduced herself as the Lady of the manor, and would he care to come in for a cup of tea?

His first reaction, he confessed, was terror. There was this extraordinary creature – 'like some great multi-coloured, crested bird', her flaming red hair topped by a hat like a peacock's harem, a bright orange fur-lined cloak thrown over a violently embroidered skirt, the overall effect an Egyptian goddess – gazing at him with *positive anxiety*, awaiting his response as if it was the most important thing in the entire world.

He was staying at the time in a house across the road, which also belonged to the Morrells, and of course he had heard tales from his fellow COs, as he called them, of the Lady of the manor, well-known pacifist and non-conformist and a few other things besides. Hence, he said, his terror.

So he followed her dutifully across the muddy field

and through the portals of the grand manor into a room of panelled oak, painted red, 'like something out of *The Arabian Nights*, Rudi'. They were quite alone, just the two of them, and she sat him down and ordered tea and asked him all about himself and how he came to be a conscientious objector and what a fine and brave person he must be. He did not disabuse her of this impression. In fact her very presence and nodding approval filled him with such confidence that he soon found himself sharing intimacies with her. 'No, not those sort of intimacies, Rudi.'

He told her of his artistic sensibilities – 'What artistic sensibilities?' I couldn't help interjecting – which again met with Her Ladyship's ardent appreciation, and how his father had disinherited him as a result. He described to her his exploits with his pals in Berlin, and his passion for free-thinking. She listened with total concentration, her glorious eyes on him, with the occasionally muttered 'dear boy', or 'oh poor you'. 'Such sympathy Rudi,' Sacha exclaimed, 'and from a stranger, and a Lady to boot!'

On being questioned about his marital status he confessed he was not married nor ever likely to be, at which milady nodded thoughtfully, and then after a long pause she mentioned a clinic in, as he remembered, Switzerland, where it was believed one could go for 'treatment'.

This unexpected remark had him flummoxed for a moment and there was a terrible pause before he declared, in a voice he struggled to control, that he was perfectly happy to be as he was and to remain so; and the very mention of 'treatment' he found, actually, rather offensive, as it suggested he was ill or, worse, suffering from some kind of perversion, which he assured her he was not.

To his surprise she laughed at this and said something to the effect that, 'I suppose it does no harm,' and went on to talk about something completely different and never mentioned it again. And in any case, as he was to find out subsequently, many of Lady Otterly's closest friends were, as she herself cheerfully acknowledged, 'sodomites'.

He claimed he became quite a confidant of Her Ladyship and was even invited to stay weekends in her house, often when she was not there, and to become part of her social set, which comprised, apart from the Prime Minister, some of the most important writers and thinkers in the country; people like Bertie Russell and D H Lawrence and the Woolfs, and all those artists – Duncan Grant and Mark Gertler and Carrington – the house was *dripping* with them. Such a miraculous collection of eccentrics and free-thinkers, 'I was in *heaven*, Rudi.' They were pacifists to a man, or a woman, and full of praise for his courage in making a stand. He was never made to feel out of place, quite the opposite. He was treated not just with the greatest respect, and interest, it was to him, he claimed, that Her Ladyship turned when one or other of her so-called 'friends' offended or insulted her. 'Which, Rudi, you'd be amazed, and dismayed to hear, was quite often.' It was surprising how these same friends who so enjoyed her hospitality, as she was without doubt the most generous hostess in the country, laughed at her behind her back and even considered her a figure of fun.

Naturally I didn't believe a word of it. I told Sacha I thought much of it was exaggeration, not to mention self-fulfilment, bearing in mind his ambitions to hobnob with the Bloomsbury set.

'Very well,' he said, 'I will prove it to you. I will engineer an introduction to Her Ladyship herself.'

'We'll see,' I replied.

<h1 style="text-align:center">21</h1>

When I was eventually able to get a word in edgeways I told Sacha of my own wartime experiences chauffeuring VIPs between top secret locations, dodging the Zeppelins, often in the dead of night, usually at a moment's notice and frequently without headlights. Of how I became friendly with politicians such as Lloyd George and military leaders like Kitchener – some of it slight exaggeration as I never actually met Kitchener, though I did become quite chummy with the delightful Lloyd George, and I was damned if I'd let Sacha steal all the limelight. And how, in my own way, I had made what I considered to be an important contribution to the war effort.

He pretended to be unimpressed. 'But you didn't manage to stop the war, did you?'

'No more nor less than you did.'

Then I told him about Fred. That sobered him up.

'I'm so sorry Rudi, why didn't you tell me?'

'I'm telling you now.'

He looked genuinely distressed, and embarrassed, unusual for Sacha.

We walked home in silence, which was unusual for both of us. I asked him where he was staying and he shrugged, so I told my housekeeper Janet to make him up a bed and said he could stay as long as he liked, so long as he didn't boss me around or heaven forbid criticise anything I did. He feigned innocence, and surprise. 'Would I ever do such a thing, Rudi?' And so began one of the more bizarre episodes of my bizarre life.

I think we were both in a kind of limbo. Along with so many others, the war had consumed us so completely than once it was over we found ourselves thinking – now what? My job had ended and I was in no rush to find another. Fred had left me enough to live on and with my widow's pension, and the house, I was comfortable enough.

I was more worried about Sacha. He was both homeless and unemployed, and suffering from malnutrition, which was not uncommon after the war for people of no fixed abode and therefore no way of acquiring food through a ration book, or by any other means. But it wasn't just food my queer friend was lacking. Something had knocked the stuffing out of him.

When you think back to that terrible war to end all wars it wasn't just the millions of young men who'd made the ultimate sacrifice, it was what the war did to the survivors that made one wonder whether mankind wasn't a mistake.

I'd seen some fierce women in my time, not least among the suffragists, even though at that stage their fierceness was kept under tight control. But I don't believe any woman would take a country to war at the drop of a hat in the way our male leaders did back in the day. The very notion that the winner is the one who manages to kill the most – 'the most' invariably meaning the ordinary private soldier; not the general or the admiral, but the lad who used to deliver the newspapers or bake the bread – has to have emanated from a man. When one thinks how victory is handed to the bullies, over and over down the generations for ever and ever amen, it is no wonder wars keep happening.

The damage that war did to the Sachas of this world, the conscientious objectors whom society spurned and spat at and strew with white feathers, condemning them as cowards and traitors and not fit to be human beings – these were ordinary people, men and women, turning on each other in a way that made my heart weep. I wished I'd been there at his side when those holier-than-thou nobodies rained insults down on him. I'd have told them a thing or two. I'd have told them if there were more Sachas there'd have been no war in the first place, and those husbands and sons and fathers and brothers they mourned would still be alive and doing useful things rather than leaping over trenches to be mown down like cattle.

Sacha was unusually quiet for the first few weeks as my house guest. Looking back, those were the bright days, the days when we weren't at each other's throats, when it was all dutiful concern on my part and a kind of subdued thoughtfulness on his. He spent most of the day in a deep fug. 'Just thinking,' he responded to my gentle enquiries. 'Just ruminating, Rudi.'

One morning, a propos nothing in particular, he asked me outright what it was, out of all the men I'd known, that made me pick Fred as a life partner?

He had met Fred, of course, and I don't think he'd been impressed. My husband had none of the quirkiness or the complicated sexuality of the sort of men Sacha went for, such as his chums in Berlin. Fred was too normal for the likes of Sacha. So what was it about this frankly ordinary man, was what he was really asking, that I found so appealing?

This was not a question I had ever asked myself and I didn't know how to answer it.

'Was it the sex?' Sacha asked, as Sacha would.

'No, not particularly.'

'I thought you loved sex. I thought sex was one of the most important things in your life.'

'That's frightfully rude and presumptuous of you darling; of course I like sex, but there are other considerations.' I thought back over my life fleetingly. Mikey and Denis and all the others were racing past me, like riffling pages of a book, so quick I could barely identify them.

'I liked Fred,' I said.

'You *liked* him?'

'I'm not sure I really liked any of the others, now I come to think of it. I couldn't imagine waking up in the morning with them beside me, day after day, too horrible for words. Is that a bad thing?'

'I'm not passing judgment,' said Sacha, with what looked to me like a highly judgmental frown.

The circumstances of my first meeting with Fred played a big part, I always knew that. If you first set eyes on another person when they're hopping around on a station platform like a crazed stork, one shoe on and one shoe off, and you don't immediately run in the opposite direction, that's not a bad beginning. If Fred was not completely put off by my loss of dignity then the likelihood was he would take any further indignities in his stride; which he did, as did I. And finding the same things funny was an excellent way to build a rapport. Meeting people at smart events when we're all dolled up to the nines and on our best and most artificial behaviour is a terrible way to start any kind of relationship. Had Fred and I encountered one another in any other circumstances, things might have turned out very differently. But we didn't, and so they didn't, and that was as much self-analysis as I was prepared to undergo.

Sacha asked me if I mourned Fred, and when I didn't immediately reply he said he thought I was a much deeper person than I made myself out to be. That underneath the superficial banter was a woman of wisdom and feeling. As always with Sacha I was never quite sure if he was having me on. So I told him, of course, yes, I thought about Fred, and had a little weep now and again. But what upset me most was not knowing exactly what had happened to him. And, now you come to mention it – excuse my sniffles – it was the sheer waste, of his life, of so many other lives, and for what? Why did nobody ever tell me exactly how he died, or where, or whether they ever found his body and if they did, what happened to it?

I was sobbing quite openly now, like a small child, dribbling and snuffling, shoulders heaving. I thought I'd got that off my chest with Claudia that time, but it seemed it only took the smallest dash of sympathy to set me off again. And so Sacha pulled me to him and held me while on it went, this terrible sobbing, my body jerking and shaking like a demented mechanical doll, till I was exhausted.

I took to my bed then and stayed there for two days. Sacha poked a head around the door now and again asking if I required sustenance, as he put it, which I didn't. I was too tired, and really all I wanted to do was go to sleep and not wake up. Which is not the same as wanting to die; it's to do with not having the energy to carry on.

On the evening of the second day I managed to stagger downstairs to be greeted by a dining table laid for two along with table mats, napkins, my best silver – *where did he find that?* – and a couple of candles stuck in bottles posing as candelabras.

He'd made soup, Sacha pronounced proudly, out of pretty well everything he'd been able to lay his hands on in my pantry. I found a bottle of ancient claret that was truthfully past its best and on this we feasted, and drank toasts to drown our sorrows and the taste of the soup, and laughed, and cried a bit. And then Sacha told me his plan.

We were going to visit the Front, he said, to find out exactly where it was that Fred had died, and how. I looked at him for a moment, boggle-eyed. 'Gracious,' I said, 'where did that idea come from?' He said Fred's ghost needed laying, I needed to know he didn't die in vain, or even if he did, I needed to know that too.

I told him it was a terrible idea and in any case, how would we go about finding the wheres and the whens and so forth? He said this would not be a problem. We'd begin with my colleagues at the War Office, it couldn't be that difficult, and then we'd jump on a train and go there to see for ourselves. His eyes were sparkling as they always did when Sacha had found purpose. In fact I rather think that was the main motivation behind the whole crazy exercise, to give Sacha the purpose he so desperately needed. How could I deprive my dearest friend of what he so desperately needed? So for Sacha's sake rather than mine, or so I thought at the time, I agreed.

22

I began with Charlie.

Charlie – Sir Charles to most people – had been my boss at the War Office. It was his job to supervise our motley group of drivers, all of them men of course, apart from yours truly. He worked in a musty set of rooms at the top of one of those anonymous buildings near Whitehall. We had no trouble gaining entry to the building – do anything with enough confidence and no one questions you. I walked into his office and greeted him with a smacking kiss on the mouth (as I always did), at which he shot back on his chair as if he'd been stabbed (as he always did), before harrumphing into his moustache and muttering, 'Oh, it's you again'; and then, after another harrumph, during which he remembered his manners: 'How are you?'

I told him I was a lot better thank you since I'd seen him last, due to the fact I was no longer working for him. In normal circumstances I might have been surprised to see him still sitting in the same leather chair in the same dismal office – Didn't you know the war was over? I might have said. But Charlie was one of those permanences around whom the world revolves. I half believed he'd been born in that very same chair and I was quite sure he'd die in it. What he did in it meanwhile was a secret only known to him.

He looked at me in his doleful fashion and asked what was the purpose of my visit, was it to see him? No, he didn't think it was. I introduced Sacha and explained our mission. Charlie frowned and scratched his chin and stroked his moustache and harrumphed some more and muttered something about the Official Secrets Act.

I was ready for that. The first time I'd encountered the Act, through Fred, I was ridiculously thrilled, and foolish enough to think it was glamorous. But ever since I began my driving career it had become a thorn in my side, in all our sides, us War Office minions. It was dragged out every time we asked a simple question about anything, its sole purpose to keep us in total ignorance throughout the whole proceedings. I wasn't having any of it.

'This is my husband we're talking about,' I reminded him. 'Official Secrets Act be damned.'

He muttered something more about certain operatives being still operative and I said I understood that perfectly, but I wasn't interested in other operatives, I was concerned only with my late husband. And in any case whatever secrets he allowed himself to divulge would remain secret, he knew that. Hadn't I been his loyal employee for four years?

'All I need is a name,' I said. 'If this room is bugged you can write it down, while pretending to go on refusing me, how's that?' I cocked my head and tried to look winsome. 'Otherwise,' I went on, as innocently as I could get away with, 'we could just, you know . . .'

I mimed opening a drawer. Sacha was staring at me in incomprehension. When Charlie didn't immediately react I repeated the gesture, this time with sound effects. He got it then.

He scribbled something on a notepad, tore off the sheet and handed it to me.

'You'll find him round the corner in Whitehall,' he said.

'Top floor. Tell him Sir Charles sent you.'

'Thanks, Charlie.' I gave him another smacker, this time on the cheek. He managed a weak smile and watched us blearily as we made our exits.

'What was that about?' Sacha demanded the moment we were out of earshot. I told him there were things I knew about Charlie that he would not want made public, such as the bottle of Johnnie Walker he kept in his desk drawer. I'd caught him at it quite early on, but I'd loyally kept my mouth shut.

'So this is blackmail?' cried Sacha, with delight.

'If you like,' I said.

'Ripping!' Sacha beamed. 'Straight out of *Thirty-Nine Steps*!'

I had to remind him we were on a serious mission here and not to get carried away.

The scrap of paper had a one-letter name on it and an address. Sacha was right, it was beginning to look like something out of a spy novel.

'His name's S,' I said.

'S for . . .?'

'S for S.'

S's office was on the top floor of yet another nondescript ministry building. His secretary greeted us with a guarded smile.

'I've come to speak to S,' I said, with some authority.

'May I ask your name?'

'Prudence de Vere. My husband Fred – Wilfred – used to work for him.'

She waited for more. I cleared my throat.

'I'm on a mission . . . this is my brother-in-law Sacha Mountview, by the way.'

'Hello, Mr Mountview.'

'Hello.'

'We are on a mission to find out what happened to my

husband. He died in 1915.'

'I'm so sorry.' She put on her serious face. 'How do you think Mr – S – might help you?'

'I was told he could.' She waited. 'Sir Charles told me he could.'

'You know that all information on overseas operatives is classified, Mrs de Vere.'

'Yes, dammit, I spent four years working for the War Office. I don't want to know what they got up to, though it would be interesting, I grant you that. I just want to know what happened to my husband. Is that so strange?'

'I could look him up in the files if you like. Though I doubt very much I will find anything that isn't . . .'

'Bound by the Official Secrets Act. Yes yes yes.'

She was making no move towards the files, wherever they were, or to anywhere else. I sat down across the desk from her and looked her straight in the eye.

'Did you have a good war, Miss . . .?'

'Chambers.'

I'd guessed she was a Miss and I'd guessed right. She was forty at least, nearly my age. She wore a grey cardigan buttoned up to the chin and poking out beneath it one of those horrible flowered blouses favoured by spinsters of a certain age, in an attempt to make themselves look younger. She had a tiny mouth that she'd tried, and failed, to make look bigger with lipstick. Now even I know that playing with lipstick is a knack, and she did not have it.

'I expect you're glad it's all over now though, aren't you Miss Chambers, so you can get on with whatever it is you have to get on with.' It was a statement, and she inclined her head and said nothing, fair enough.

'Me too,' I rambled on. 'I was a driver for the War Office you know, the only female driver on the team.' I paused. She gave me a tight little smile. 'It was exhausting. And I don't just mean the work itself, that was enough. It was the secrecy, you know, not being able to say *anything*. It's unnatural to spend so much of one's time and energy doing something and then not being able to tell anyone about it, don't you think? By way of conversation, for instance. What else does one have to talk about over the dinner table?'

She went on sitting there, still with that tight little smile. She reminded me of someone . . . oh yes, it was the policeman I'd been confronted with all those years ago, in the days of the suffragists. She was using the same trick – keep mum and the other person will get bored soon enough and bugger off.

But I wasn't buggering off anywhere. I said, quietly and, in my view reasonably, 'You know, I don't have much to do today, so I am going to keep sitting here until I get to speak to your boss. I don't mind waiting. I'll come back if you like. I'll come back even if you don't like. I . . .'

'Perhaps we could make an appointment.'

This was Sacha. An *appointment.* I gave him my best glare and then I stood up and leaned right over the desk towards Miss Tightlips, as if to exclude my stupid friend who seemed only too happy to be fobbed off.

'This is really of vital importance, Miss Chambers. As a woman I'm sure you understand this. Did you lose anyone in the war? Hmm?'

I could hear a gasp from behind me. Miss Tightlips looked startled for a moment.

'I believe there was an uncle . . .'

'I'm sorry to hear that. How did it happen?'

'He . . . I'm not quite sure. He was an officer with the – er . . . On the Somme, I think.'

'You think. Did they find a body?'

'Rudi . . .'

'I never asked, I . . .' She was looking positively frightened now, and upset, which was the intention.

'Just suppose he had been your husband, and he'd disappeared off behind enemy lines without you knowing, or without anyone telling you, which isn't the same thing, and the next thing you heard he'd been killed, though how or where or indeed why, nobody is prepared to tell you. How do you think you would feel? Would you just shrug your shoulders and carry on, or do you suppose you would want to know more? If not while the war was on, but afterwards, do you think you might do all you could to find out everything, or would you comfort yourself knowing everything was hush-hush thanks to the Official Secrets Act, in which case . . .'

It was at this point that the inner door opened and the poor woman, who was looking so terrified by now that even I was beginning to feel sorry for her, leapt to her feet as if she'd sat on a firework.

'Hello hello hello,' said a male voice. 'Heard voices, thought I'd see what was going on. Can I help you?'

It was me he was addressing. He was a ruddy-faced, cheerful-looking man, stocky, with huge bushy eyebrows. His remark was said kindly and so I immediately replied, 'Yes, you can. Are you S?'

He chuckled. 'Yes, I am S. Who is it wants to know, might I ask?' He was looking from me to Sacha with an amused smile.

I introduced myself, and Sacha, and at the mention of the name de Vere his great eyebrows shot up and he said, 'Wilfred's better half! How delightful to meet you! Come in, come in. And you too.' This to Sacha.

Resisting the urge to blow Miss Tightlips a raspberry I followed S into his inner sanctum.

23

'Sit down, sit down, please.' S hunted about him for chairs and arranged them around his desk. 'So very good to meet you after all these years, Mrs de Vere.'

We took our seats either side of his massive desk and he gave me a beaming smile.

'Well, fancy this. Wilfred's wife. Can I offer you anything? Tea? Coffee? We have both,' he announced with some pride.

I shook my head.

'Now I'm not just saying this, Mrs de Vere, but Wilfred was one of our best operatives, without a doubt. The best. Not just because you are sitting here opposite me. A remarkable man.'

'I'm glad to hear it,' I offered politely.

'Did he tell you how we first met?'

'He told me virtually nothing at all.'

'I'll never forget it. He conducted the entire interview in German.' S chuckled. 'I was asking him the usual, you know, where born, brought up, schooled, etcetera, in English of course. He responded in German. To every question. My German is scratchy to say the least but I knew enough to know he was answering my questions, in fulsome detail. But what was even odder, remembering I'd never met this man before – he'd been recommended to me by a colleague who knew he spoke fluent German . . .'

S leaned over the desk and lowered his voice. 'The man he was describing was born in Hamburg, educated in the local school, which he named. I checked it out later, the school existed, and so on. But it wasn't him.'

I stared at him. 'What do you mean, it wasn't him?'

'Was he born somewhere like Hamburg, Mrs de Vere?'

'He was born in Bognor Regis. Or so he told me.'

'Precisely.' S sat back in his chair and started to guffaw.

'I'm not sure I follow you.'

'I'm not surprised!' S's shoulders were heaving. 'Felt much the same myself. He kept it up throughout the whole interview, not a twinkle. Presented himself as German born and bred. You could not see the join, I swear to you. Afterwards I said to my colleague, I told him this man who was supposed to be Wilfred De Vere had presented himself to me as Hans Something-or-other, Hamburg born and bred, and do you know what he said? "Stuff and nonsense," he said. "He was playing a game with you".'

S sat back in his chair and there was a silence. This was Fred he was talking about?

'I still don't follow you,' I said again. 'Are you saying he was playing the part of a native-born German? What for?'

S looked at us and all but whispered, 'To convince me that he could pass for a German, behind enemy lines.' He chortled. 'And it worked! How it worked!'

I was speechless. This was a side of Fred I'd never known, and I could not picture this at all.

'You look puzzled, Mrs de Vere, as well you might. I've met some cards in my time in the Secret Service but never one like Wilfred de Vere.'

'So he went behind enemy lines,' I stammered. 'And that's where he died.'

S inclined his head ambiguously.

'Was that a yes or a no?'

'It was a classified maybe, Mrs de Vere. You understand . . .'

'About the Official Secrets Act. Now listen to me, Mr S.' I was on the edge of my seat now and almost wagging my finger at him. 'I spent just a few precious years with Fred keeping my mouth shut.' I ignored the snort from Sacha. 'I didn't ask him how he spent his day, or where he'd been. If he was sent away somewhere I didn't ask where he was going, for how long, nothing.' I wasn't quite sure where my line of thought was going so I changed tack. 'Have you ever lived with a spy, Mr S?'

He waved a hand in the air.

'No, of course you haven't. It isn't like normal life you know, not being able to discuss your work with your nearest and dearest. It's a bit like living with . . .' I couldn't immediately think what it was like living with, I was fumbling rather. 'It requires a lot of trust, more than an ordinary marriage. For all I knew Fred could have been spending his days cavorting with exotic dancers in night clubs.'

Sacha laughed aloud at this. S went on staring at me seriously, and sympathetically, but silently. I took a deep breath.

'And now that he's dead, I believe you owe me something. Having kept the faith for so long, for my king and country and so forth, much as I hated the war and everything it stood for, I – need – to – know – what – happened – to – my – husband.' I was stabbing his desk with my finger now.

'Mrs De Vere.' He was speaking so softly, and bending so far across his massive desk towards me I thought for one alarming moment he was about to grab my hand. 'I understand every word you say, and I am sympathetic to the core, believe me that. The fact is . . .' he paused. 'I do

144

not know where or how he died.'

'Then who does?'

His turn to take a breath.

'A letter of the alphabet, don't tell me. P. Or O. O for Obfuscation.'

He sighed. 'Actually it's F.'

In any other circumstances I might have laughed. Spy novel indeed.

'F was stationed in Belgium. He was the coordinator for our occupied territories operatives. He would be the one to help you, only unfortunately he died.'

I stared at him. 'You mean he was killed too?'

'No. Spanish 'flu. Six months ago.'

'I don't believe you.'

'I assure you it's true. I would not lie to you, Mrs de Vere.'

'And he's the only person who knows what happened to Fred?'

He didn't answer this.

'That can't be true. I know enough to know there are checks and balances, there have to be.'

'One thing I can do for you, Mrs de Vere.' S paused, and did a strange thing. He winked at me. It was so out of place I thought for an instant it might have been a nervous tic. 'I can ask around,' he added, unsatisfactorily. 'That is all I can do.'

'That's very kind of you,' said Sacha. 'We are very grateful. Come on, Rudi.'

'If you'd care to leave your contact details with my secretary I will get in touch if I find out anything.'

He looked sincere enough, poor man.

I felt suddenly exhausted.

'Thank you,' I said, getting to my feet. I shook his outstretched hand. 'And I'm sorry to be so . . .'

'You have not been in the least so . . .' He smiled

kindly. 'Your husband was a very brave man. And a lucky one.'

I suppose that was meant as a compliment. But I couldn't see how anyone could describe Fred as lucky.

S escorted us out of the room and spoke briefly to Miss Tightlips before bidding us a warm farewell. I very nearly didn't bother to give her my address. I could see nothing but brick walls stretching from here to infinity, every one of them labelled with a letter of the alphabet.

24

On our way home on the bus together, Sacha and I, we discussed the wink.

Sacha pronounced it a gesture of great significance. I said I didn't think so, I thought S was just playing games with me. Sacha said he was not the sort of man to play games and if I was implying he was flirting with me, well nothing could be further from the truth.

I said I wasn't implying anything, and in any case what was wrong with a bit of mild flirtation? Or did he think I was past that kind of thing?

Sacha responded that I was deliberately misconstruing his remark and that it only showed, yet again, how fixated I was on the whole topic of flirtation, and how incapable I was of conducting a normal relationship with a man without thinking they were flirting with me.

I said that was absolute nonsense and proved he knew nothing about me. This utterly ridiculous argument continued throughout the journey and for some time after we arrived home, by which time neither of us could remember how the argument had begun in the first place. Childish though it seems in retrospect it served to deflect me from my main concern: that the man I married was not who I thought he was. Or rather that the man S described, the 'German' with the complete and meticulously researched background, was not the Fred I knew. To think that he might have spent his time in the war impersonating a German, living and fighting among them, struck a chill into my bones – I couldn't quite explain why. It's a known fact, now, that the soldiers who fought in the trenches were so traumatised they were unable, or unwilling, to describe their experiences to their families back home. It's a lesser known fact that this gap in understanding caused the breakdown of a number of those same relationships. If Fred had survived the war, would our marriage have survived it as well? Would he have shared his war with me?

I tried to explain all this to Sacha but he told me once again I was over-dramatising, that the men who fought in the war were not the same men who went about their daily business harmlessly both before and after it. I was not convinced.

Then came the letter. It was addressed to Mrs Wilfred de Vere and it stated simply, *I knew your husband Mr de Vere and I would like to call on you at your convenience.* It was signed 'R for Reginald'.

R for Reginald. It was becoming more and more like something out of fiction. I was on the verge of tearing up the letter when Sacha grabbed it out of my hands.

'Don't you see?' he cried. 'The wink!'

I went blank. 'The wink?'

'That was what he meant, S. He meant he was going to help us but he couldn't be seen doing it. Or heard.'

'How can you be so sure?'

'By trying him out. Getting him over here, this R for Reginald, and seeing what he has to say for himself. I'll be here to make sure you he doesn't rape you or flirt with you. Or worse, not flirt with you.'

Very funny. I gave Sacha my best glare, but I rather thought he might be right, so I wrote back to R for Reginald to say yes, I would be ~~prepared~~, ~~happy~~, interested to see him this coming Thursday or Friday morning any time after 11am.

I half expected a German acting under a British pseudonym, but the R for Reginald who turned up on my doorstep two days later was unquestionably British – what Fred would have termed 'a Cockney sparrow'. He was little taller than me and carried himself bolt upright, military fashion. His hair was fair and his tiny eyes twinkled. I resisted the urge to address him in Cockney rhyming slang.

R had also been an agent working behind enemy lines, in Belgium, that much he was able to tell me. Wilf, as he called him, or 'Hans', his code name, had so successfully passed himself off as a German that Reginald, who had been primed to meet up with a British operative one dark night in March 1915, was not at all sure he had the right man, despite the name and the exchange of a complicated system of codes. The initial meeting was followed by others, at intervals and always in different places and times of the day, during which Fred/Wilf/Hans would pass on information about German plans and movements, in code, of course; information which, according to Reginald, was 'dynamite'. An unfortunate word to use, I thought, in the circumstances.

If I struggled to see Fred as a German I struggled even more to see him as a regular soldier. As far as I was aware he'd had no training, but then nor had many of the fighting men, on either side, volunteers or conscripts, not until the war broke out, Reginald explained. When I asked how the strange impersonation came about, R replied that it was entirely Wilf's idea as far as he knew – it was certainly not 'regular practice'. No one else, he remarked cheerfully, would have the 'bloody nerve to go fraternising with the Hun as if it was the most natural thing in the world.'

I thought then how horribly lonely it must have been, for Fred. It was one thing not being allowed to tell his wife, or anyone else, what his work involved, and quite another to be living among the enemy, day and night, knowing that one false note, one small slip, meant the firing squad at dawn. One little glance at a photo in his wallet – for didn't all soldiers carry photos of their sweethearts, wasn't that compulsory during the war? And in that case, who was I? Was I Prudence de Vere, or was I a gentle *Hausfrau* called Bertha keeping the home fires burning back in Hamburg, or wherever it was? – that's all it would take.

I had to smile, not at the firing squad, but at the thought of Fred chatting about me with his German friends, as I was sure he would have done. I wondered what he'd said about me. He'd have had to be inventive, to create a brand new person to fit the image in the photo; not the clumsy little Englishwoman who caught her heel in grills on station platforms, who fought for women's right to vote and drove ministers of His Majesty's Crown along dark roads in the Home Counties. I hoped he'd told them I was a nightclub singer in a dive in the red-light district of Hamburg, or an exotic dancer at the *Fols de Rols* in Paris, last seen entertaining the occupying German troops. Oh, but I'm hardly of an age to be doing those sorts of things any more, I had to remind myself.

'He was a right one, was Hans,' said R, with a grin. 'Never knew anyone like him. Always joking, even right in the middle of the sh . . . of the worst of it. Always with a smile on his face and "How's the old C?"'

'"Old C"?'

'He was the boss. Actually the boss was K but he called him C for . . .' He stopped. 'Anyway, he made you feel it was all a bit of a game – a boys' game, you know. He was a right joker, was Hans.' He shook his head.

I didn't think we were getting very far. I wasn't completely sure about 'R for Reginald'.

'Isn't the whole point of calling someone by a letter of the alphabet so nobody gets to know anyone's name?' I asked him. 'In which case doesn't "R for Reginald" sort of give the whole game away?'

He laughed himself stupid at that. 'You could say, yes, only nobody ever called me that.'

'So what *is* your name?'

He looked at me in surprise. 'Reginald,' he said.

It was turning out to be a long morning, so I thought I'd cut to the chase and ask him straight out, 'How did Fred die?'

At this Reginald's chirpy smile vanished. He scratched his head and pulled a series of facial expressions and then he said, 'Look, I don't really know,' in such a way that made me believe he knew only too well.

'Why can't you tell us?' I asked him, as kindly as I could.

'Because you don't want to know,' he began, before correcting himself. 'You think you do, but you don't. You really don't. What good does it do at this stage, eh?'

Well, of course my hackles were up now.

'If you're trying to save us from something nasty don't worry about it,' I said. 'Nothing is worse than not knowing. Can't you understand that?'

'Of course. But you see I don't. I don't know.'

There was a pause. He was shifting uncomfortably in his chair. Poor man, he didn't need to have come here, he didn't have to have communicated with us in the first place. But here he was now, and no doubt he'd said more than he'd meant to. Too much, but still not enough as far as I was concerned.

'I have to know, Reg,' I said, adding an edge that I hoped was mildly threatening. 'I won't sleep easy till I do.

I may not sleep easy when I do, but I have to know. I will know.'

I thought for one awful moment that perhaps, just perhaps, R for Reginald had killed Fred himself. Wasn't that what happened to agents who were at risk of being discovered by the enemy? I heard the rumours that they carried cyanide pills with them – anything to avoid passing on information under torture.

'Did he kill himself?' I asked.

'Crikey no, why would he do a thing like that?' Reginald snorted, with embarrassment I thought. He was beginning to wriggle in his chair now, like a naughty schoolboy.

'If he'd been caught, and faced torture, wouldn't he commit suicide rather than give the game away? Isn't that what spies are meant to do in those circumstances?'

'Well, yes, sometimes. But no! No, he didn't kill himself.' There was a pause. It was my turn to act mum to get him to spill the beans. Reginald glanced up at me and a look of horror came over his face. 'You don't think I killed him, do you?'

'Until told otherwise, that is what I was thinking actually, yes.'

'Blimey.' He looked from me to Sacha and back again. He was scared now. 'I would never have done that. Why would I ever do that? Oh no, Christ no.'

'Then who did?'

The poor man was almost in tears. But I knew he knew. Before he wrote me that letter he must have realised what I needed to know above all else: how, where and why did my husband die?

After several minutes of silence during which poor Reg sat with his hands clasped and head hanging, he looked up and said, 'Look, I'll tell you what I'll do. I'll get in touch with K.'

K, otherwise known as C. From bad spy novel to French farce.

'He was in charge of the agents in that part of the . . . over there. It may take me a while, I don't know where he is. He may still be there for all I know.' Reginald paused, thinking, then he said, 'Yep, that's what I'll do.'

I'll pass the buck, is what he was saying.

'Are you telling me you don't know what happened, or that you do know but you don't want to tell me?'

'Rudi.'

I looked at Sacha and he gave me a warning frown. 'What?'

He gestured at Reg, whose head was almost hanging on the floor now.

'Where might we find this K?' I asked him. It wasn't that I didn't trust him, but I had a feeling that once he walked out of that door R for Reginald would want to put the whole business behind him and forget he ever came here.

'He was in charge of agent operatives in the . . . in the Brussels region, Brussels north.' He said all this quickly and quietly and without looking at me. There was a pause before he added, 'Flemish. Speaks English with an accent like . . . like . . .'

'Like a Flemishman.'

'Bang on.'

I took a breath. 'Anything else? Distinguishing features?'

'He had this – sort of darky skin. I don't mean like a darky I mean like a . . .'

'Dark skin?'

'Yes, but not African.'

'Mediterranean.'

He nodded vaguely.

'That's all I remember. And . . .' He stopped.

'Yes?'

'Well, if you do catch up with him, don't mention my name, will you?'

'But I don't know your name.'

'Well, yes, you do.'

'You mean you really are Reginald?'

'Well, yes.' He looked at me, and then at Sacha, frowning. It's then that I burst out laughing, as did Sacha. And then, not sure what he was laughing at but probably because he was relieved that after all perhaps he stood a chance of getting out of there alive, Reginald joined in.

I laughed till my muscles ached, I have no idea why.

25

After that I went into a blue funk. I tried to suggest to Sacha that we make the pilgrimage to Belgium in search of 'K'. But as he pointed out, two foreigners wandering around the continent looking for someone known as 'K' – though only to others working in the secret service, who were either dead or still bound to secrecy, even if we could find *them* – stood as much chance of success as an elephant walking a tightrope.

But having got so far, for Sacha to run out on me was beyond the pale. Especially since he was the one who'd sparked my interest in the first place.

'Think of something!' I yelled at him. Yes, yelled.

'Like what?' he yelled back.

'I don't know, there must be a way.'

The worst thing about uncertainty is the way you fill in the gaps.

Reginald's reluctance to tell me how Fred died was ominous. It meant, as I saw it, either his death was nasty, brutish and long, or that he'd died in some kind of disgrace. The third option, that Reginald was trying to protect someone else, did not occur to me, as even an optimist like myself can believe the worst when the truth is kept so tightly secret. After the war there was plenty of talk of heroism and sacrifice, and just occasionally of cowardice, or what was viewed as cowardice but in my book was more likely plain common sense. But most of the dark secrets of the war were kept secret until some time later. Nobody wanted to spoil the feeling of relief, and celebration, that accompanied the peace.

I began having nightmares. Fred in front of a firing squad. Fred, wounded, floundering in mud, desperately trying to crawl away from gunfire. Fred under interrogation, tortured, screaming – try joking your way out of that, sweetheart. Fred up there somewhere smiling down at me, mocking me and my feeble attempts to get at the truth. Worst of all, Fred miraculously turning up on the doorstep, unharmed, a case of mistaken identity. How cruel it was to wake up to reality from that.

I decided to make some enquiries among my erstwhile colleagues at the War Office. Most of them were still working there. There was Stan, who was in charge of the vehicles, and Ernie, whose job I never quite understood but could best be described as a 'runaround' – it was these sorts of people, the so-called workers, who were far more likely to know things than their supposed superiors, because they were usually brighter and kept their eyes and ears open. Further up the career scale were Linda and Harry, junior clerks. Harry could be promising, I thought. He'd been forced into the job by his father, also a civil servant, had no aptitude for it, did not take it seriously and was notoriously indiscreet. The only problem with Harry was that like so many people working for the government he was terrifically well bred and tremendously stupid.

They were all very sympathetic and eager to help. Harry had a pal who worked in a bar in Berlin who he claimed 'knew everything', which was the kind of thing the kind of person like Harry would say. Linda had an uncle who'd spent most of the war in Belgium doing something or other, she wasn't quite sure what but she could try to find out. Most people had cousins or brothers or uncles who'd at some point fought in or went to or visited the occupied territories. It was all terribly vague and in the end none of it went anywhere.

Then Stan mentioned something to me about a man he'd met at the beginning of the war who he thought might have had something to do with the secret service. 'You can always spot them,' he pronounced. It was to do with the manner in which they spoke to you, and looked at you, the way they asked 'casual' questions that were in fact quite probing; how they pretended to be not particularly interested in their surroundings when you could see their eyes took in *everything*. 'The thing about spies,' he went on, 'is how ordinary they are. The more ordinary the better. Forgettable, you know, so if someone was to ask you to describe them you couldn't. You couldn't pick on a particular feature like a large nose, or a boss eye, or whether they were very tall or tiny, or anything.'

Like Fred, I thought.

But there was one thing about this particular man that made him stand out, said Stan, and that was his complexion. Not Arab, not Eastern, more like a – you know, someone who spent a lot of time in the sun.

'Like a Mediterranean?' I was interested now. 'Who was he?'

Stan didn't know, he was never – as he put it in a pretend posh voice – 'introduced', which is partly why he became interested in the man in the first place.

'Could his name have begun with a K?' I asked.

He shrugged, as if to say he had no idea and in any case, names were interchangeable, not to say exchangeable. K one day, L the next, who knows?

Mediterranean Man made several appearances at the beginning of the war, which was reason enough for Stan to remember him. He wasn't working directly for the War Office – Stan would have known if he was – but he got the impression he was someone to be reckoned with. Even the top brass listened when he had something to say.

It was sounding more and more promising. But Stan was in no position to make enquiries, and so what, he'd come across this man many times before the war but never once the war started, which was significant in itself. But he had no idea who he was or what happened to him, and no way of finding out.

I thought about broaching Charlie again but rather thought I might have shot my bolt the last time, with the threat of blackmail. Still it was worth a go.

I shouldn't have been surprised when Charlie refused to see me. I was hurt, as Charlie and I had been close friends once, as I saw it. I also thought he owed me more than a scribbled name and an address on a scrap of paper; in fact the more I thought about it the more I realised I'd been fobbed off between government departments. It was classic civil service behaviour to pass on the problem to someone else, in the hope that the troublemaker (who was me) would give up in the end and quietly go home.

But they hadn't reckoned with Prudence de Vere.

Stan promised to 'ask around' and see what he could come up with. So did Harry and Linda, not to mention Ernie, who probably knew more than any of them, as it was his job to run errands between departments; though I doubt very much he understood the purpose of either the errands or the people who were setting them.

I could see the usually friendly faces of my former colleagues beginning to cloud over every time they saw me, which was several times a week by then. Somebody, deputed no doubt by Charlie, had the effrontery to ask me what I thought I was doing hanging around the department since I no longer worked there. I didn't dignify this with a reply. There's a time for being a nuisance and a time for quitting, I knew that, and I wasn't prepared to quit.

But then other things cropped up, fortuitously, to turn my mind in a quite different direction.

26

First, my mother died.

She slipped out of the world as quietly and inconspicuously as she had lived in it. It was a wonder she had kept going as long as she did, there was very little left of her in the end.

I felt a kind of loss, but not the loss of losing someone so much as the loss of never having really had them to begin with. Apart from the odd occasion, such as those few weeks when we mended clothes together, laughing and vying with one another to be the most inept seamstress who ever graced the planet, we never really did get to spend much proper time together.

My father went into a kind of trance. At the funeral I tried to take hold of his hand by way of comfort, but he wriggled away from me with embarrassment. It was a step too close to intimacy in our family. He sold the house and went to live with Toby and his family, and I didn't see much of him for the eight months or so before he too departed the world.

So a significant period of my life came to an end. I was an orphan. I had moved further up the ladder towards death. It was my turn next, you could say, so there was no point in hanging about.

~

Because that is how it felt, after the war, for so many of us women. A giant, almost tangible feeling of Now What?

Women's groups were springing up all over the country, initiated by those doughty souls who'd done so much to keep the country going while the men were shooting the hell out of one another. Having proved through their achievements that they were equal to men in every respect they thought it was high time the outside world woke up and recognised it.

Probably the largest and best known of these assemblies was the Six Point Group. They comprised a bunch of strong-minded females, many of them ex-suffragettes, with a set of Serious Purposes. I can't remember all six of them offhand but they amounted to demands for equal opportunities for women, at home and in the workplace, pensions for widows, rights for single mothers and all that sort of thing.

I was invited to join one of these groups by a friend called Lizzie, whose husband had also died in the war. They called themselves the 'merry widows', she said, and they met up every so often in tea rooms or somesuch, to chat about this and that. I told Lizzie I was not one for the company of women as a rule, the suffragists notwithstanding, and the last thing I wanted to do was to sit in a room with a bunch of gloomy widows crying into their teacups. My friend, who you could well describe as a 'merry widow' as she had visibly blossomed since her widowhood, assured me it was nothing like that, so I thought – Nothing ventured, and so on.

We were not as determined or as campaigning as the Six Point Group, needless to say. We did start out with Serious Intentions, but somehow discussions on important topics such as universal suffrage or rights of inheritance became sidelined by the latest gossip concerning Mrs Stopes' book *Married Love*, or what effect the death of the corset was having on female morality. What we did have in common with the doughty women was our refusal to be considered 'superfluous', simply because thanks to the lack of worthwhile young men as the result of the war single women outnumbered single men by something like two to one. And if you were not a wife or a mother you were considered surplus to requirements.

The merry widows were a motley mix of sizes, ages and types, though we were not all widows and not everyone was as merry as my hostess or myself. We'd all lost someone close to us in the war – husbands, sons, brothers, uncles – or so it was presumed rather than spelt out loud. But then who hadn't in Britain at that time?

There were among others a terrifyingly aristocratic woman called Celia Bluntly-Sythe, who was, comically, even more ashamed of her name than I was of mine. 'Besides *no one* ever spells it properly', she was fond of repeating. There was a serious egghead called Florence, who'd studied the classics at Cambridge and who never cracked a smile; an angry man-hating woman called Fee and a cheery, brazen soul called Valerie who, it was whispered, made a living as an artist's model. She was probably brighter than anyone else in the room, Florence included. There were others whose names I never did manage to remember. And there was my chum Lizzie, who found life in general a total hoot, despite having lost her own (much older) husband.

The one thing we never discussed was the war. It was almost as if that was a taboo topic; which was why, when Florence made her announcement, it came as all the more of a shock.

She told us she'd attended a talk given by a man named Sir Arthur Conan Doyle, who, she informed the ignorant among us, was one of the leading writers of the day and the creator of the legendary detective Sherlock Holmes. The talk was not to do with literature or medicine however but the afterlife, which Sir Arthur seemed to know a great deal about through a practice called spiritualism, otherwise known as communication with the dead.

Now I'd heard of spiritualism. My mother had mentioned it at one point when she wanted to get in touch with her father after he died to find out where he'd hidden his will. It sounded pretty fantastical to me, and had it been anyone other than clever Florence I would not have given it serious thought. But Miss Bluestocking, in her measured, aloof way, had quite obviously fallen for it, or more to the point perhaps for Sir Arthur, and such were her powers of persuasion that when it came to asking for volunteers to attend a séance, with a proper medium, I felt my hand go up.

I kept my hand raised, along with two or three others, while Miss Bluestocking did a quick count, nodded, made a note on a pad and then announced: 'Right then, we meet at my house on Thursday week, seven o'clock in the evening.'

It was at that point that Valerie let out a loud and unmistakable 'Ha!'

Florence whipped round and, staring directly at her, barked, 'Who said that?'

Valerie smiled broadly and declared the whole thing to be hokum and trickery; anyone with a brain in their head knew as much.

Florence, her hand on her hip, which jutted impressively, then demanded to know what made Valerie assume she was cleverer than the well-known novelist Sir Arthur Conan Doyle, not to mention the brilliant Alfred Russel Wallace, the not quite as well-known biologist, now deceased, who actually arrived at evolutionary theory before Darwin.

Valerie then embarked on a long tale about Conan

Doyle and Harry Houdini, the well-known escapologist, and how they'd become bosom friends until their very public falling-out when Houdini described Conan Doyle as delusional, in public. 'Just because a person makes a living as a writer,' she added finally, with a striking cock of the eyebrow and a smile that could cut through steel, 'doesn't mean he's intelligent.'

There was silence from the rest of us in the room as the two women batted the argument back and forth between them, like a tennis ball. Two fantastically brainy women, each with an equally compelling argument, it seemed to me, and like the best arguments you start out agreeing with one side and then you switch to the other. So I, and others with me, found ourselves cheering first for Florence: 'How you can take the side of a cheap entertainer over a man of letters is beyond me!' and then for Valerie: 'Entertainer maybe, cheap certainly not, and there's nothing to beat insider knowledge!' and then for both sides simultaneously. This went on for some time until Mrs Bluntly-Sythe finally got to her feet and with a voice that shook the rafters called out, 'Ladies, please!'

There followed a long pause as both women turned to stare at Mrs B-S, who then announced: 'There is only one way to resolve the argument, and that is to arrange this *séance* as you call it and see what happens.' Then she smiled sweetly at us all and resumed her seat.

So that got quite a hum of excitement going, as you can imagine, and now women who had not yet put up their hands did so until I believe everyone's hand was in the air, including Valerie's. Florence nodded decisively, as if that in itself had won the argument for her, while Valerie sat looking on at us all with a mixture of pity and amusement. Lizzie giggled and said 'What larks!' and slipped her arm through mine.

I was mightily intrigued. It so happened that Sacha had

seen Houdini perform in a packed theatre in London a few years before, and marvelled as he escaped from locked caskets and handcuffs, often when suspended upside-down, and sometimes in water. I remember remarking at the time that I could think of many things I'd rather spend my money on than watching a man escape from handcuffs, but it could be quite a handy skill if he ever got in trouble with the law and had to break out of gaol. Which, Sacha said, he had already done, by way of experimentation.

Valerie, it turned out, had actually met Houdini and said he was the cleverest person she had ever come across. He had what she called a 'native cunning', and being a trickster himself he was always on the lookout for other tricksters. He knew how to crack the secrets behind other people's tricks and, if he thought someone was up to no good he didn't hesitate to expose them. The rift between him and Conan Doyle came about after a séance conducted by Doyle's wife and attended by Houdini, during which Mrs Doyle appeared to conjure up the spirit of Houdini's late and much-loved mother. The only problem being she had the woman communicate in English, a language which Houdini claimed his mother never spoke in her life.

It was a right laugh, said Valerie, to think it was Conan Doyle the wordsmith who believed in magic and the supernatural while Houdini the self-made entertainer debunked the existence of either of them.

For myself I'd back the word of an entertainer, cheap or otherwise, over a man of letters any time. But there's always that tiny niggle of doubt that tells you you're too dim-witted to understand these things, that ghosts only appear to people who have extra-special powers of perception and so on. So when the day of the séance came I found I was filled with a mixture of curiosity and terror.

What if there was something in all of this? What if I did come face to face with Fred and he was horribly scarred, perhaps with bits of him missing? Did I really want to put myself through that? What if he told me he'd died slowly, agonisingly, in huge pain – did I really want to know?

'Pull yourself together,' I said to myself. 'It's all hokum.'

~

So come Thursday evening there we were, all fifteen of us (I counted), clustered together around Florence's dining table on a chilly November night. It was dark outside, and pretty dark inside come to that. A lit candelabra stood in the middle of the table and a couple of dim lamps had been placed on the sideboard. The medium was a tall, majestic woman who went by the name of Mrs Barbaraski. She was dressed for the part just as you'd expect, in ruby-red velvet with mauve and aquamarine shawls, and embroidered mittens – a nice touch – and pince-nez. She waited while we sat ourselves down and ceased our chatter. Our faces around the table, lit by the candles, were appropriately ghostly. She looked at us over her pince-nez and then began to speak in a voice so quiet you had to lean forwards to hear her.

'There will be disbelievers among you.' There was silence as she looked around the table. 'But for this séance to have meaning,' she paused, 'for what we are setting out to do, I ask of you, for this evening only, for just two hours of one evening, to put your prejudices to one side.'

Prejudices?

'Open your minds and throw out all the chaos of your lives. For the next two hours there is nothing except what is in this room. These people. This table, these chairs. Close your eyes and open your minds.'

We did as bid. I opened one of mine enough to take a quick look around.

'All of you.'

And shut it again quick smart.

'Be aware of your breath.' With eyes shut you had to concentrate all the more to hear her. 'Be aware of your body, of the weight of your body, of gravity pulling you towards the ground. Feel your feet on the ground, the weight of your feet anchoring you to the earth, supported by the earth. Without the earth we cannot exist, and without us the earth would not exist.'

There was another slight pause, during which I tried to make out whether or not I agreed with the statement about the earth not existing without people on it, and whether without anyone on it it was provable one way or another.

'The spirit world is not part of the earth world. The spirit world exists on another plane, at a higher vibration. Spirits are made of light and energy. Take a deep breath and allow your body to fill with white light.'

White light. Whatever that meant, I couldn't feel myself filling up with it.

'Feel the lightness of the spirit world above you. Imagine your body growing lighter in the white light.'

Then she began to croon, in a deep, soothing voice. I wondered if she might be lulling us to sleep. It was a pleasant sound. I could feel my heartbeat slowing.

The crooning then changed into a low, rasping noise. Then it stopped.

'If there is someone there, show yourself.'

I opened my eyes a slit and realised the room had gone almost completely dark.

'There is someone there, I can feel you. Show yourself. Don't be afraid.'

I felt suddenly cold.

'Who is it?'

Someone in the room started to sob.

'Who is it?' Her voice was strong now, commanding. 'I ask you to show yourself. Are you known to anyone in this room?'

The voice, when it came, sounded far away.

'I am.' It sounded male, needless to say. Fred?

'What message do you have for us?'

There was no answer.

'Spirit!' She was in full sergeant major mode now. 'Declare yourself! Who are you?'

There was a low murmur, I couldn't make it out.

'Is this your message for us?'

A pause, another murmur. My eyes were fully open now and I realised someone had somehow snuffed out the candles on the table. The only light seemed to be coming from a single lamp on the sideboard behind me. It took a while for my eyes to adjust, but all I could make out were shadows, and Mrs Barbaraski leaning back in her chair. I looked around for the source of the male voice but it was too dark.

Just then I felt a sudden draught, as if someone had opened a window, though there was no sign of one. I felt it waft past my face and across the table and away.

'Fred?' I had spoken aloud, but as I thought, very softly. I closed my eyes again, to concentrate better. I felt something brush against me and I sat stock still, rigid with terror and excitement. I could swear there was someone standing right by me but I knew if I opened my eyes he, or she, would disappear, so I kept them tight shut and remained motionless. There was the faintest waft – was there? – of tobacco, of Fred's tobacco, and an enormous and unexpected feeling of calm. I smiled, and I found myself not wanting the moment to end.

But it did end. It ended rather abruptly. The lights snapped back on and when I opened my eyes I found the whole room was staring at me, and Lizzie was trying to suppress a laugh. What had I done? Mrs Barbaraski was smiling at me with such love and gratitude I was horribly afraid I had fallen for her trickery just like Sir Arthur, which filled me with confusion and not a little dismay.

It appeared I was the only one who came away from the evening with a sense that something had happened in that room. Even Florence had to admit to feeling nothing in particular. She defended Mrs B to the limit, she was one of the best apparently, but that was the whole thing about the spirit world: sometimes spirits appeared, sometimes they didn't, there was no way of controlling them. 'If there was,' she babbled on, 'we could all do it, we could all be mediums. All we'd have to do is sit in a dark room and chant and up they'd pop.'

I thought Florence was talking a bit too much, defending herself against an attack that had not materialised.

'But Prue saw something, didn't she?' said Valerie, with an encouraging smile.

I looked at their faces. It was a week after the séance and I was only just now getting back to any kind of normality. I didn't want to admit it, not in public at least, but the whole experience had affected me quite a bit and I didn't know why. If you asked me to be completely honest I would have said I did feel a presence, a real one, and the reason I knew it was real was because I didn't think I had the imagination to conjure up something that wasn't.

But I wondered if it hadn't simply been that I had so desperately wanted to sense Fred's presence, and it was that want that was responsible for my confusion. That was all it was. I began to see Conan Doyle's point of view. If you've ever experienced it you know that something has happened, no matter how ludicrous or irrational it sounds. It felt real even if it wasn't.

But I was embarrassed. Yes, unembarrassable me did

not want to admit my true thoughts to anyone.

I avoided the merry widows for a while after that. I didn't want to be made to feel more of a fool than I already was, and I especially wanted to keep out of the way of Florence, who had a mad look in her eye.

27

I made the mistake of telling Sacha. He looked at me in disbelief, then threw his head back and laughed for a whole minute. He was laughing so much it took him some time before he could form a sentence.

There was no proper response to that. I felt hurt, humiliated, and angry – with both him and with myself for saying anything.

'Sorry, Rudi,' he said, eventually.

I scowled.

'You of all people, Rudi, imagine! There's just no telling what you'll come up with next. How is it in the spirit world?'

'I don't want to talk about it.'

'But you must! Not many people have had the privilege of experiencing the afterlife. Did you feel enveloped in white light? Did you meet St Peter? Or is it St Paul who's in charge of the pearly gates?'

I had no intention of responding to this, and in time Sacha gave up, but not before he'd apologised again and then ruined it all by bursting into laughter yet again.

Fortunately, for my sanity and for our friendship, a couple of days later Sacha received an invitation from Lady Utterly Otterly to attend one of her famous 'Open Thursdays', at Garsington, and he was welcome to bring along a friend.

I was tempted to say I was too utterly uninterested, not to say busy, to be bothered with the likes of Lady Otterley. But frankly I felt in need of a change of scene. So I went.

~

'She's not what you'd call a woman's woman,' Sacha warned me. 'And watch out for the maid, Millie, she's Otty's spy.'

'So she's "Otty" now, is she?'

We were on a train down to Garsington in Oxfordshire, the dreary, tranquil English countryside zipping past us on this dull spring day.

'She'll probably be perfectly pleasant to you though. She won't see you as too much of a threat.'

'Thank you darling, that makes me feel so much better.'

'Don't be like that Rudi, I meant it as a compliment.'

Sacha's compliments were unique to him, you could say. Still, if nothing else a trip to the countryside, which is not something I generally go out of my way to seek, was a welcome distraction.

Nobody who moved in post-war London society could have failed to have heard of the famous Lady Ottoline Morrell. She was known for hosting house parties, first in London and now in her country pile in Oxfordshire, attended by the leading lights of the cultural and political world. And while she was neither an artist nor a politician herself she managed, by the way in which she attracted such an opposing mix of people and obtained their confidences, to wield quite a lot of power and influence in certain circles.

Lady Otty was married to a man named Philip, who was a member of parliament, but she was rumoured to have dallied with a number of other men, including Bertrand Russell and possibly even D H Lawrence, who according to Sacha had an astonishingly violent aversion to homosexuals and had once spoken to him in a highly threatening manner.

It all sounded like the best fun, even allowing for Sacha's usual exaggeration. After a month's cohabitation with him there wasn't much I didn't know about Lady Otty. I was anticipating someone with a booming voice and a frightening demeanour, who made a point of seducing every man she met – Sacha and his like excluded, of course – and patronising every woman. I was predisposed to dislike her intensely.

What I was not prepared for was Garsington Manor itself. I dare say Sacha had described it to me but I was either not listening or he did a paltry job of it.

I've always found Cotswold stone rather depressing. It's all very well to wax poetic about how it glows like gold in the sunshine but frankly, we don't get a lot of that in this country and so for the most part it looks like what it is: drab and grey, and everywhere. Garsington was Cotswold stone from top to bottom, but for some reason the overall impression, even on this damp spring day, was neither intimidating nor dull.

It was set in what you'd call a typical English landscape of trees and lakes and rolling fields with cows in them, the sort of scene that sends the hearts of poets and artists and Americans aflutter. The house itself stood behind huge wrought-iron gates leading into a cobbled courtyard. The Morrells, my guide informed me, had transformed Garsington into an 'Italianate paradise'. But it was the view from the far side of the house that took even my breath away. A large sloping garden led down to a lake surrounded by classical statues, and beyond it was an orchard and more fields – it was a working farm, as my friend and guide constantly reminded me – and to cap everything: peacocks.

We were greeted at the door by the famous Millie, who like the best spies appeared quite run-of-the-mill and no more interested in us than one would expect. She led us into a hallway dotted with Chinese artefacts, and from there into the very drawing room that Sacha had described: wood-panelled walls painted what he termed Venetian red, comfortable-looking furniture and a huge fireplace. And everywhere the smell of potpourri.

There were around a dozen people in the room, mostly men, a surprising number of them young. They formed two distinct groups – the younger at one end, soberly dressed, and the not quite so young, or formally clothed, at the other. The lady of the manor on seeing us extricated herself from among the young men and approached us with arms outstretched, and with a 'Daaarling Saaacha' she grasped hold of his hand and kissed him on both cheeks before turning her attention on me.

She was both as I had expected and as I had not. She had short bobbed hair which was rather obviously, though not unpleasantly, dyed auburn. Her rather striking nose protruded from a face as pale as milk, which was heavily – though again not crudely – painted with crimson lips and dark shadow around the eyes. She wore a long sapphire-blue flowing dress and a bright red shawl, and around her neck were several strings of pearls. The overall effect was remarkable and eccentric, but all of a piece.

She shook me most warmly by the hand and assured me she knew all about me, and I almost believed her.

'What have you done to your hair, Otty!' cried my companion, rather cheekily, but her response was amused, and unoffended.

'Bertie told me I was going grey, darling,' she stage-whispered into his ear. 'So I thought it was time I did something about it.' Then she chuckled, and tucking a hand under each of our arms she brought us further into the room and introduced us.

The young men it turned out were undergraduates

from Oxford whom she had invited in order to discover 'how our future is looking'. The middle-aged man lurking on the edge of the group and looking decidedly ill at ease was her husband Philip, who welcomed Sacha like an old friend. Lady O then steered us on to the other little gathering and introduced Clive, John, Aldous and Brett and a couple of others whose names I didn't catch. Clive and Sacha greeted one another with open arms, and while the others nodded a vague hello and then turned to carry on their conversations I was left with John.

The most remarkable feature about John was his moustache, behind which his mouth was completely hidden. But there *was* a mouth, because from it emerged a cheerful 'A new face! How wonderful!' He then went on to denounce most of the people in the room, especially those he had just been in conversation with, as 'middle-aged and worn-out and with nothing new to say', but in a manner that was more comical than disagreeable and made me warm to him immediately.

It transpired that Clive was Clive Bell, a fellow conscientious objector whom Sacha had befriended during the war when they were both living over the road in Home Place. Aldous, who peered out at the world through inch-thick glasses – I later learned he was almost blind – was the author Aldous Huxley and Brett was, well, Brett, female and very deaf.

I knew them all of course, by name at least, thanks to Sacha and those endless evenings during which he regaled me with every fascinating detail of the extraordinary private lives of the 'Bloomsberries' as he called them. How Huxley had offended Lady O by making fun of her by way of a character in his latest book – an accusation which he denied. Of the bizarre household of the Bells: Clive and his wife Vanessa (also an artist), who lived in a *ménage à trois* with the artist Duncan Grant, himself a homosexual, but with whom Vanessa had had an affair and by whom she had produced a daughter, Angelica, who Clive passed off as his own. Grant had had affairs with virtually everyone in trousers, according to Sacha, including my new friend John.

In the flesh these people with their astonishingly eccentric private lives seemed quite ordinary, and their conversation, though occasionally risqué, as one might expect, sounded to me often forced, not to say affected. They bandied witticisms about like weapons and there were undercurrents of competitiveness and downright malice. At one point they started laying into the recently published book of a famous author friend, who was absent needless to say, like vultures picking through the remains of something dead. When they turned to me and asked if I'd read it I was able to announce, not without some pride, that I had never read a book in my life. One or two of them gazed at me as if I were a thing from outer space, but my friend John roared with laughter and declared – 'At last! A true Philistine!' – and gave me a hearty kiss on the cheek. When I asked what a Philistine was he burst into laughter all over again and asked me to marry him.

Shortly afterwards Lady O approached me, in a friendly manner, and asked if I would care to join her in her room for a cup of tea.

I realised I was about to be interrogated, or initiated, and that this was something that took place whenever a new person appeared on her doorstep. Up the stairs we went to her 'boudoir' as Sacha termed it, a room he claimed he knew well. She asked me about my family and my childhood and how I passed my time. She listened to me quietly and attentively, occasionally offering an 'Oh my dear', when I told her about my mother, and a 'How extraordinary' when I described my chauffeuring efforts in the war. I confessed I had no creative instincts whatsoever, to which she shrugged and said, 'No more do I,' and we laughed together.

Then she started talking about Sacha and what a shame it was about his sex life, about which she seemed to know more than I did, which took me aback rather, coming out of the blue as it did. She remarked, with a sigh, that so many young men seemed to have taken to sodomy these days she had begun to fear for the future of the human race. And what a strange sensation it must be to lust after people of one's own sex, and my dear, one wouldn't mind so much but so many of them were downright *promiscuous*. 'Though not Sacha, of course,' she added. She said she had offered to take him and others of her queer friends to a doctor she knew in Freiburg, in Germany, who'd had some success in 'curing' some of the young homosexuals who came to him. Sacha, naturally, had refused – with, she added, smiling, some vehemence.

Then without preamble she asked me about my own love life, and what my sexual partialities were. Did I prefer a 'mature' man to a boy, she wanted to know, or a foreigner to a 'native'? I was unsure how serious this question was intended to be so I ran off a list of some of the lovers I had known, from Mikey onwards, accompanied by brief biographies of each and including, perhaps bizarrely, Mrs Pat. At this Lady O's face lit up and she clapped her hands together – an unexpectedly childish gesture – and exclaimed how wonderful it was to hear about such adventures and to meet a woman of her own heart! I didn't quite know what to make of this but it seemed my extensive love life, or at least my willingness to tell her about it in some detail, more than made up for my lack of artistic pretensions in the eyes of my esteemed hostess.

I have to admit she was a remarkable listener, and she had the ability to make one say more than one might otherwise have said, especially to a total stranger. So naturally I told her about Fred and about my so far unsuccessful quest, with Sacha, to discover the circumstances of his death. On hearing this she rose to her feet, strode to the door, opened it, leaned over the banisters and shouted, 'Philip! Come here!'

I heard footsteps outside and after a few moments she re-entered the room followed by her mild-mannered husband. He smiled at me and gave a nervous little bow.

'Philip will help you,' announced Philip's wife. 'He knows everyone in parliament, don't you dearest?'

'As do you,' said Philip, with a smile.

'Dearest Prudence,' Lady O placed a proprietary hand on my arm, 'lost her husband in the war, and when I say lost I mean lost.' She paused, for emphasis. 'He was a spy you see, so nobody knows what happened to him, or perhaps they do, but nobody is prepared to tell her. We must do all we can to help her.'

Her husband looked down at me and stammered something I didn't quite catch. I couldn't help thinking what an unlikely man he was to be married to a socialite like Lady O.

'Speak up dear!' she barked at him, and then turned to me and said, 'You'd never think he'd been a member of parliament, would you? And a fine one too!' At which she reached out, grabbed hold of her husband's sleeve, pulled him to her and gave him a smacker on the mouth.

'We're looking for a man with a Mediterranean complexion who went under the name of X,' she said.

'K,' I ventured.

'K. He was in charge of secret service operations in Belgium. He shouldn't be too hard to trace, should he?'

Her husband gave a little laugh and stroked his chin. 'We can but try,' he said.

'We will do more than try,' said the great lady. And

then she took hold of my hand and gave it a squeeze and said, 'We will succeed, my dear. Rest assured.'

It was all a game to her, I realised, but none the worse for that.

28

There were more trips to the country following my initiation into Garsington society, sometimes with Sacha and sometimes on my own. I was known as 'Lady O's Philistine friend', a description I was quite happy to go along with, and to exaggerate where the situation called for it. Even the Bloomsberries began to warm to me after several visits, treating me as a kind of pet halfwit or, as one of them called me, 'our Socratic stool-pigeon'. This, according to my friend John, to whom as you will recall I was by now engaged, was a reference to an Ancient Greek sage called Socrates, who in discussion pretended to be a numbskull, like me, so the issues in question were reduced to words and thoughts of one syllable, and complex arguments broken down into simple ones. Or so I understood it.

So whenever they fell into disagreement about something, the clever Bloomsberries, they would turn to me and say, 'What does Prudence think?' Then the whole room would go quiet as they waited with bated breath for the words of wisdom that issue from a child. And I would play the game with gusto. Because it was a game, I wasn't in the least offended; it was a way of assuring I was the centre of attention, even if it sometimes meant pretending ignorance when I didn't possess it.

So I enjoyed my visits to Garsington very much. Lady

O still invited me for the odd confidential chit-chat during which we would vie with one another to be the stupidest and most useless specimens known to mankind. Coming from someone who read Ancient Roman poetry for pleasure – her, not me – this was ridiculous. 'I have no talent at all,' she was fond of telling me, 'except for one thing: people.'

Which, on reflection, was the one thing we may truly have had in common.

One afternoon she summoned me to her boudoir with some seriousness, sat me down and said, 'We have to talk about John.'

She launched into a biography of my fiancé's life in intimate detail. He was 'a darling man' as she described him, funny, clever and loved by all. He'd recently written a best-selling book criticising the terms of the Versailles Treaty, I think that's what it was called. However, she felt I ought to know, he had enjoyed relationships with 'both sides', as she put it, including liaisons with bus drivers in Eastbourne and miners in Cornwall. His reasoning being, as he had explained to her quite without shame, that it was the only way an aristocrat like himself could get to understand the thinkings of the working man, which in his profession he considered invaluable. We never discussed what anyone did for a living at Garsington, it was assumed everyone knew already, except me of course. So when I asked what that profession might be and she said economics, that surprised me as I had assumed John to be an artist like everyone else; even though I could tell he came from landed stock and was a lot better dressed, not to say better behaved, than the rest of them.

That was not all, my hostess continued, almost without drawing breath. There were rumours that John had been seen in company with performing artistes, and in particular with a Russian ballerina named Lydia

Lopokova to whom, it was said, he was intending to propose.

There followed a long pause, during which I'm not sure who was the most confused and confounded: Lady O because she'd had to deliver what she thought was a bombshell to her friend, or her friend who was unsure whether Lady O was joking or, which was even more unlikely, whether she had taken my flirtation with John seriously.

She was watching my face anxiously and when I let out a chuckle she frowned, and then smiled, and then joined in the laughter with obvious relief.

I told her I already knew something about John's murky past and I wasn't in the least upset, except that it meant the end of our enjoyable flirtation. To make up for it I vowed, silently, I would get my moustachioed friend into bed one way or another before he tied the knot with his ballerina.

After we had gone back downstairs again I collared John right away and told him he owed me, and that if he resisted I would tell the whole world about the bus drivers. He told me in return that the whole world already knew about them and I'd have to do a lot better than that. I said Russians were known for their fearful tempers, especially the women and even more especially artistic types such as ballerinas, and this was his *last chance* to taste forbidden fruit before he settled down to solid married life. *Think about that!* I said to him.

All this took place right there in Lady O's crimson-panelled living room, within earshot of anyone who cared to listen, and there were quite a few of them. One or two of the Bloomsberries began to cheer me on, which wasn't quite what I wanted as John, despite his genial nature, was quite a private sort of a man, and very soon the situation began to get out of hand. So, not quite knowing what else to do I grabbed hold of John's arm and steered him towards the doorway, through the throngs of people, pausing for a fraction of a second on spotting a familiar face gazing at me in astonishment.

I kept on going and once we were outside the door we burst out laughing until we were shaking and made not for the upstairs bedrooms but straight for the French windows and onto the lawn at the back of the house, and like giddy youngsters we raced one another down the grassy slope to the lake beyond and it was all we could do to stop ourselves from tipping right into the water.

We walked on until we were out of sight of the house and sat down on a stone bench that overlooked the Berkshire Downs. I asked John if he'd ever been with a woman and he smiled but didn't reply. I said I hoped he wasn't marrying for *convenience*, or convention, or any other of those unspeakable reasons, and he sighed and said, 'Actually Prudence I do rather love the woman.' But if it mattered to me *so much*, he went on, he was quite happy to walk on until we were completely hidden from human view and then do anything I wanted to do in the shelter of the woods. I said that sounded wonderful, if a little uncomfortable, only I had just spotted my goddaughter among the young men in Lady Otterley's drawing room, and as her moral guardian I felt I should, on this occasion, forego his kind offer, even though it was no more than I deserved as the jilted fiancée.

And so, arm in arm, we returned to the house without a hair or a moustache out of place. Some of the Bloomsberries gave us curious looks and I thought – Let them think what they want, there is something else requiring my attention right now, which was:

What was my goddaughter doing in Lady Ottoline Morrell's drawing room?

'Dearest Harriet.'

I gave her a warm hug. It was like embracing a statue. She had grown into a startlingly beautiful young woman, with her pale face and huge dark eyes that peered out at me from beneath an ominous fringe. She wore a strange concoction consisting of layers of grey, orange and purple lace, very bohemian. It was a few years since I'd seen her and in those years she'd gone from gawky and grave schoolgirl to assured, and still grave, young woman.

'What are you doing here?' I asked.

She was so busy staring at me she didn't appear to hear the question. I repeated it, and she immediately drew back and waved vaguely in the direction of a young man, saying, 'Auntie Prue, this is Felix. Felix, this is my Auntie Prue.'

'Her godmother actually,' I said, holding out my hand to her young man, which he took and shook weakly, 'but hello anyway.'

I then introduced the young couple to my former fiancé, and my goddaughter looked at each of us in turn with puzzlement. The last time I'd set eyes on her I was in inconsolable tears at the sudden death of my husband and crying on her mother's shoulder, so it was not surprising if she found my present behaviour inappropriate. I thought of trying to explain the whole business but I could see it would lead me into ever deeper trouble, and the young do take things so *fearfully* seriously, Harriet especially.

So I gave a merry little laugh and released John, with a kiss on the moustache and a tweak on the backside, and turned my attention to my goddaughter.

Felix, it turned out, was an undergraduate at Oxford and this was his first time at Garsington. 'He's a writer,' Harriet pronounced, her eyes shining with adoration. He was an odd-looking fellow, languid in the extreme, his hair flopping over one eye which gave him a kind of squint. He was not the sort of man I would have expected

Harriet to go for, but then what did I know.

I asked Harriet whether she still had aspirations to be an actress and she gazed at me in incomprehension before shrugging and saying, 'Oh, that.' Which I took to mean No. I did a swift calculation in my head and realised she must be, what, twenty-two years old, give or take, so what were her plans for the future?

Looking up into the face of her writer friend she tucked her arm into his and said, or rather sighed, that she was Felix's muse. Felix gave her a lazy smile that was only just this side of dismissive, and I wondered to myself whether being anyone's muse was an appropriate occupation for a young woman, especially such an earnest young woman with aspirations like Harriet. Twenty-two was very young to lose one's ambitions, but then I never had any so maybe I didn't fully understand what it was like to have them in the first place.

'How are you getting on, Auntie Prudence?' It was a bit of a loaded question, bearing in mind my recent behaviour, and she knew perfectly well how much I hated being called her auntie.

'We struggle on, Harriet,' I said, with what I hoped was a wan smile. 'How about you?'

'Felix and I are setting up home together!' she cried, snuggling up to him, which made him wriggle with discomfort. 'We're looking for a place right now, something we can afford, which isn't much!' She laughed, shrilly.

'And what does your mother have to say about that?' I asked politely.

She shrieked with laughter, a touch hysterically. 'Who cares what anybody thinks?'

Well that was something I could identify with, obviously, though I wasn't convinced she really meant what she said. There had always been a manic side to

Harriet. She was what people termed 'highly strung', like a tennis racquet. And like a tennis racquet, things – people, chitchat, life in general – seemed to ping against her with such force she was at constant risk of breaking. I didn't like the look of Felix, who while all this was going on was studying his shoes with blatant boredom, and as Harriet's moral guardian I felt protective of her.

'Dearest Harriet,' I said, 'it's high time you came to stay again and we got to know each other.'

She looked at me suspiciously for a moment and then she said, 'Can Felix come too?'

Felix regarded me apprehensively and I stared right back at him and said, 'No, just you, darling,' at which he gave an unmistakable sigh of relief.

<h1 style="text-align:center">29</h1>

Harriet never did come to visit. The next time I heard from her mother she had shut herself in her bedroom following the break-up with Felix and was vowing to become a nun. Poor child. I know it doesn't help to say I told you so, but you wonder sometimes why we can't see ourselves the way others see us.

I had bought myself a car and named her Rosie. She was sporty, and bright red, with seats very low to the ground which made her seem even racier, and I fell in love with her at first sight. I took to driving around London just to show off, sometimes with Sacha but more often not, because frankly his snide remarks about my driving, coupled with his white face – he was sick after our first trip – got on my nerves. Rosie wasn't the easiest creature to control and I did get very close to a post box on one occasion, or maybe two, but once I got the hang of her there was no stopping me. I would often take her out for the day simply for the fun of it, not knowing where we were going, or why.

That is partly why I invited myself down to the Faradays, to introduce Rosie to Claudia – she wasn't impressed, as I should have known she wouldn't be – and to catch up with my closest friend and her three graceful daughters.

Claudia and I, as many people have been at pains to

point out, could not be more unalike. Friends have wondered out loud, and quite rudely, what it is that she sees in me. They rarely wondered the other way round. I have retorted back that I am the fire in Claudia's belly and she is the serenity in mine, which sounds wonderfully poetic. Meaning that we each provide for the other what we lack. Unkind friends have accused me of riding in her glorious shadow, or words to that effect, and there may be some truth in it.

Claudia married a dullard and produced three wholesome girls, and they lived in happy chaos with dogs in a large and comfortable house called Hallywell in leafy countryside a manageable morning's drive from London. With her husband out of the way for long stretches of time you could say her life is perfect, though if it were me I would be dying of boredom. As a mother she is calm, naturally, and loving in her way, and allows her girls to do more or less what they want so long as it doesn't annoy her guests. The one thing that stops her being Little Miss Perfect is what I can only call a lack of drive, a passivity, as if she expects the world to come to her rather than she to it. Some people claim she lacks confidence, though why the Girl with Everything should feel a lack of anything is beyond me.

I pity any child who is brought up under the straitjacket of a woman like Claudia who never shows her feelings or knows how to act impulsively. I mean this in the nicest possible way, you understand. Claudia wouldn't see it like that of course, and woe betide anyone who dares to criticise a mother! Despite that, her girls are charming creatures, in their very different ways, and have always regarded me as a kind of exotic, badly-behaved aunt who dares to say and do everything their mother does not. To fulfil this role to perfection I have been known to invent a past that's a little more colourful than it actually is, with strings of affairs with everyone from royalty downwards. I once, in my cups admittedly, ventured to the eldest girl Jessica that what her mother needed above all else was a lover, it would liven up her life no end. This had the poor girl in such paroxysms of mirth that ever since then she bursts out laughing the moment she sets eyes on me.

But I meant it. It is difficult to describe how infuriating it is to have a best friend who is always so well-behaved. I have never seen Claudia looking less than immaculate, and elegant, in her reserved and, now I come to think of it, old-fashioned way. Sometimes I think she is old before her time, but that's another thing – she doesn't even have the common decency to look her age. She has never grown plump, like most normal middle-aged women, like yours truly. She never trips up steps or catches her heel in the grills on railway station platforms. The only saving grace is her hair, a naturally dark brown but just beginning to show signs of grey. Yet even that adds to her a sense of distinction rather than age.

It's not that I hate her, or despise her, or want to be like her, although I have felt all three at one point or another, as I'm sure she has in return. We both know we would die for one another, if we didn't kill one another first.

~

As my goddaughter, of course Harriet was my main concern at that time. My plan had been to have a quiet talk with her and persuade her to come back to London with me, away from her stifling surroundings, and perhaps to find some nice young men to introduce her to.

But I'd missed the boat. When I first approached her with my most sympathetic, godmother-like smile – she had emerged from her room by now, needless to say – it was almost as if she had forgotten about Felix. There was already someone else, a friend of Felix's called Leonard, who was a poet, she said, with the same kind of adoration with which she had described Felix as a writer. And they were going to be married just as soon as she could talk her mother and father round.

It was, as Claudia explained to me later, a 'rebound reaction' on Harriet's part, not just to the ending of her romance with Felix but to the fact that her elder sister was on the point of announcing her engagement to a chap named Jonathan. It was typical of Harriet, that she should regard romance and matrimony as a competitive sport. I ventured it might be to do with thwarted ambition, and when Claudia raised her eyebrows at this I shrugged as if to say, 'What else is there for her?' Of all the three daughters Harriet was born out of her time. Privately I wondered whether it might have to do with a desperation to get away from the boredom and safety of the family home.

When Claudia refused point blank to let Harriet come back to London with me, Harriet threw one of her tantrums and retired back to her bedroom with the predictable door slam and refused to speak to anyone, myself included. I apologised for causing a family row but Claudia smiled graciously and said it was for the best, that she'd forget about this poet in due course just as she'd forgotten about Felix, and about pretty well every other passion she'd ever nurtured in her young life. I could see there might be some truth in this, but nonetheless I felt for Harriet. Of all of them – Jessica, who was endearingly silly and laughed at the slightest thing, and Flora the youngest, who was fluffy and soft and wise – Harriet was the one who stood to suffer the most in those cosy surroundings.

Then I told Claudia about Fred, and K, and the continuing mystery of Fred's death. She listened in silence, and when I'd done she said, 'Good gracious.'

'Good gracious what?'

She blinked. 'I had no idea.'

I told her it was Sacha who'd set me on this path in the first place and if it hadn't been for him, Fred would have rested peaceably in his grave. That's if he had one. That's if he hadn't been left to rot – or worse, and more likely, if he hadn't been blown to bits like so many others so there was nothing left of him to be buried, their remains instead strewn over the fields of Flanders, fertilising the grass. All those wasted lives commemorated by rows of crosses, symbolic only, not marking graves, stretching into the distance as far as the eye could see.

'Then you must go,' Claudia said gently.

'Go where?' I blinked.

'To wherever it was. Belgium.'

'Belgium's a big country.' Actually it isn't, even I know that, but you know what I mean.

'How else are you going to find your answer?'

She was right. It had been months since I'd last mentioned Fred to Lady O, or anyone else, and I'd heard nothing. Nothing at all.

'Just go,' she went on. 'To somewhere, to Brussels, and ask around. It's the only way. I'd come with you if I could.'

'Then do.'

She started to shake her head, and then stopped. She looked at me and I looked back at her and then we both broke into a smile, which turned into roars of laughter. At which point Jessica appeared and stared at each of us in turn, then joined in, and it was several minutes before she stopped, wiped her eyes and managed to ask, 'What are we laughing at?'

'Your mother and I,' I said in a shaky voice, 'are going on an adventure.'

30

Of course it never happened, the adventure. Claudia got cold feet, as I knew she would. Harriet was in a highly volatile state and Claudia was afraid if she left her alone for a moment she might elope with her poet.

So I took myself off, and away, on my own. I toured the cities of Europe, some of them, usually in the company of an organised tour from which I escaped from time to time when the mood took me. Back home I lunched or dined with friends most days and tripped to the theatre a couple of times a week. I had not forgotten my first love, the delicious Mrs P. She had married again and was appearing in the revival of a play called *Pygmalion*, written for her by a strange Irishman named George Bernard Shaw – who, it was rumoured, was enamoured of her, as were we all – playing a flower girl of all things, and she approaching her second half century if I calculate correctly.

Life went on, as life does.

Since Fred died I did not go looking for a replacement. I never thought I would meet anyone who would put up with me in the way Fred did. I was prepared for a lonely life in my old age but not for a dull one. It might have been jolly to have teamed up with the John Maynard Keyneses of this world but I always knew that was unlikely. It wasn't his aristocracy, nor even his liking for young men, nor because he was such a brainbox. It's because despite

192

my bragging and my tall tales I know my place.

But then a girl gets to a certain age – all right, middle-age – with half her life behind her and wondering what to do with the rest of it.

So I decided to sell the house and find somewhere smaller. Sacha had fallen in love again and told me he was leaving to set up home with his new 'chum', another ne'er-do-well who liked to call himself an artist. 'You're never too old to chase your dreams, Rudi,' he was fond of saying.

I had no dreams, as he knew well. I have no time for dreams, at best they're a distraction and at worst their only purpose is to make a person feel bad for not achieving them. By definition a dream is just that, an unachievable fantasy. Sacha's whole life was the chasing of dreams. Well, each to his own.

So I moved into a snug little space in Pimlico. Two small bedrooms, a cosy sitting room, kitchen and bathroom just the right size. After the family home, or what was intended to be the family home in Fulham, I could feel the walls closing in around me, enclosing me, embracing me. Just me. No maids, no companions. The clutter of the past all went. It was just me and Rosie sitting patiently outside the front door like a loyal dog. I was about to be living on my own properly for the first time in my life.

~

Then one day I arrived home from one of my jaunts to find no fewer than three wedding invitations on my doormat, from the three Faraday daughters. The first was Harriet, to Leonard, her poet – how that came about I could not imagine – followed by Jessica and her would-be politician Jonathan, and lastly darling Flora to a fellow named Carlos Something-or-other too Spanish and long-winded to possibly remember.

As for Harriet, my goddaughter, I felt obliged as the keeper of her moral soul to be introduced to her intended before her marriage. I was also burning to know how she managed to get her parents to accept a poet for a son-in-law. So I took them both to dinner at a charming and frighteningly expensive place near Leicester Square that serves the most divine Dover sole. Leonard turned up in a corduroy jacket and trousers that looked as if he'd been doing the gardening in them. He had ginger hair and an untidy beard and dirty fingernails, and announced that this week he was a vegetarian and couldn't stand the smell of fish.

It was not a good start to the evening. I could forgive the corduroy jacket, even the fingernails, but the rudeness of his manner took my breath away. He turned his nose up at everything I offered him, indeed at everything that splendid restaurant represented. I'm not sure he wouldn't have turned his nose up at the Lyons Corner House, just to be annoying.

Harriet's eyes barely left his face the whole evening. She clutched onto his sleeve, his hand, at one point the collar of his jacket in order to pull his beard towards her and bury her mouth in it, in full view of the other diners. She told me he was the most divine poet that ever walked the earth and even had him reciting some of it at one point, which he did in that awful droney voice poets adopt when reading their own work, as if the stuff is sacred. It didn't mean much to me, needless to say, but I was polite enough to nod and murmur something appropriate.

The only thing I could find in favour of the man was that unlike her previous *amour*, the bored Felix, Leonard did seem if not equally at least partly smitten by his intended. As well he should.

'You know you are marrying a remarkable girl,' I told him.

Normally I might have muttered the odd word of warning to any young man who was brave enough to take on the moody and, let's face it, changeable Harriet. I would have felt it my duty to warn them of her passing passions, the hots and colds of her temperament, always anxious, eager to please one moment, bored the next.

But in Leonard's case I felt he needed taking down a peg or two. I apologised for submitting him to such a *bourgeois* establishment – never mind that tables had to be booked *weeks* in advance, unless you were a personal friend of Maurice, the *maitre d'*. He responded by announcing cheerfully that it was perfectly all right, it was rather entertaining to see 'how the other half lives', as he put it, and he admitted that he only decided to become a vegetarian five minutes before he arrived, just to amuse us. Putting aside his bizarre sense of humour I had him down as a small boy who hadn't yet learned how to behave like a proper grown-up. The only people he spoke to properly were the waiters, and I didn't much like the way he looked at some of them, either. I wondered whether he behaved in such a way with the Faradays. I couldn't see Gerald putting up with him for a moment.

At the end of the evening when Leonard disappeared to the lavatory, Harriet grasped hold of my hand and said, 'What do you think, Auntie Prue?'

I told her I thought he was the rudest person I'd ever met in my life.

'Yes, he is, isn't he?' she responded, eyes shining.

'Tell me, how did you manage to talk your mother around?'

She stared at me blankly for a moment.

'The last time I saw you she was refusing to have him in the house.'

She broke into a smile. 'Oh yes, that. Well,' she shrugged, 'I threatened to kill myself if they wouldn't let us marry.'

'You did *what?*'

It may or may not have been true, I wasn't able to press Harriet any further because it was at that moment that her beloved reappeared at the table, rubbing his (presumably unwashed) fingers through his hair in order, I found myself supposing, to clean them.

~

I invited myself down to Hallywell a few days before the wedding, to help out, whether Claudia wanted me to or not. Gerald, over from Africa or wherever he was working at that time, stood around scowling like a disgruntled bulldog at all the toing and froing, muttering, 'What do you intend to do with all these flowers? Are we opening a nursery or something?' When I asked them both what they made of their future son-in-law Gerald grunted – he did a lot of that – and Claudia sighed and murmured something about Harriet being terribly in love and who were they to stand in her way. I told them of our disastrous evening at Monsieur Jacques and she said, 'Yes, that's more or less how it was the first time I was introduced to him. So rude,' she added, with a laugh. 'But he soon got bored with that and after a while he began to behave quite normally. And anyway,' she cocked an eyebrow at me, 'I thought Auntie Prue believed children should be allowed to do what they want.'

I pulled a face, and admitted to myself if not out loud that she had a point.

The wedding was a triumph, as it was bound to be, Harriet looking like a princess and Leonard behaving almost like a proper human being. I even caught Gerald looking on with something like fatherly pride and thought perhaps he did have a heart after all, underneath all the grumpiness.

There was hardly time to draw breath before wedding

number two, featuring the lovely, bubbly Jessica and her would-be politician Jonathan, a merry soul with a loud voice and even louder laugh, who made ridiculous jokes that only Jessica understood. Gerald was absent for that one, as he was for the third and last: the celebration of the marriage of sweet Flora to her incomprehensibly-named Spaniard.

Such merriment. Such jollities. 'Clever old you,' I said to Claudia, 'getting rid of three daughters in one year.'

She appeared not to have heard me.

'Did you hear what I said?'

She nodded, not looking at me. She was far away, as she tended to be these days, not quite with us. Who knows where her thoughts had taken her.

It was a few days after wedding number three and I was packing up Rosie ready to return to London when Claudia asked me to stay on for another night.

'The house is going to seem so empty.' She sounded almost pleading.

Speaking personally, as a woman without children, the prospect of a large empty house all to myself, with no one to question me or demand what I was up to sounded like paradise. I know plenty of mothers who do little other than complain about their children and exclaim how they can't wait for them to leave home, only to complain even more when they do exactly that. I can only suppose you have to be a mother to know what it is to be a mother.

So I did stay on for one more night. And we spent a soulful evening together, Claudia and I. I asked her at one point where she was and she stirred and said, 'What did you say?' I told her she'd drifted off somewhere; it was as if she wasn't in the room at all. She smiled and murmured, 'Yes, well.'

I asked her if she was thinking of Dougie. There was a pause and she said, 'Who?'

'*Who*?'

'Oh, Dougie.' It was as if she had no idea who I was talking about. 'No,' she said, still addressing the middle distance. 'To tell the truth I'd forgotten all about him.'

Oh yes?

'In fact,' she turned her attention back to me, 'I don't even know if he's alive. I've heard nothing of him for so long.'

But she must have wondered. Lord knows, I had. I'm not even sure I didn't still harbour just the teeniest bit of a fancy for Dougie. He was a wonderful lover after all, one of the best.

I was about to voice these thoughts out loud but an unexpected flash of wisdom told me not to. Not then, anyway.

31

I pondered on Claudia all the way home. I was concerned for her. Her loneliness was palpable, especially after all the fun and games of three weddings, and she cooped up in that big house all alone, I could see that. But I was annoyed too, because knowing Claudia she would do nothing about it. I could invite her to stay with me for a while but I didn't think for a moment she'd accept, and *that* was what annoyed me more than anything.

But the moment I stepped through the door of my little place in Pimlico the whole business of Claudia went right out of my mind. Waiting for me on my doormat was a letter inviting me to tea at I's teahouse in X Street near Piccadilly at four o'clock the following Wednesday. It was signed, *Anna. A friend of K.*

If I say I had quite forgotten all about K, and my attempts to discover what happened to Fred all those years ago, it wouldn't be altogether true. Having tried everything I could think of to solve the mystery and gotten precisely nowhere, I had worked hard to put it out of my mind and get on with my life. And right up until this moment I thought I'd succeeded.

So as I stared at the letter I felt my blood run cold. My first instinct was to ignore it. I almost threw the letter away. My second instinct was to telephone Sacha, who happened to be at home and who insisted on coming round right away.

He was thrilled. 'Of course you must go!' he yelped. He was dancing around the room like a small child. 'This is a breakthrough! This is the real thing!'

I couldn't see what he was basing those assumptions on. I told him at best it was a practical joke and at worst I might be kidnapped or who knows what. He told me he could see no earthly reason why anyone should want to kidnap me, not at my age, and certainly not in broad daylight in the middle of Piccadilly; but if I was that concerned he would come with me and lurk in a corner.

'You will never forgive yourself if you don't go!' he exclaimed. 'Just imagine in years to come, when you're old and incapacitated and unable to do anything except sit in a moth-eaten armchair and ponder on your life and think – If only I'd taken Sacha's advice that time, at least I'd know what happened.' I told him I had no intention of becoming old and incapacitated, and why did he assume my armchair would be moth-eaten? To which he expostulated that yet again I was deliberately avoiding the issue and that despite all outward appearances I was actually a coward.

There was a bit of a silence following that. No one in my life had ever, *ever* accused me of cowardice, quite the reverse. I was the one who rushed in where the rest of the world feared to tread. It had been my stock in trade, if you like, not to say my undoing on more than one occasion. But the problem was, at that moment, he was absolutely right.

The silence lasted a good two minutes and was broken by Sacha, who spoke so softly I could barely hear him.

'The worst that can happen is it turns out to be a waste of time. The best that can happen is you know the truth, that your late husband was a war hero.'

'You can't know that.'

'He died, didn't he? Cowards don't die. Cowards run. Only the brave stand and fight, and sometimes die.'

It was becoming all too melodramatic for words. In the end it was to appease Sacha as much as anything that I eventually agreed, and made him promise that if I hadn't called him by, say, seven o'clock on the day he was to call the police. He vowed to do anything, 'anything you ask, Rudi,' so long as I kept the assignation.

~

Come the day, I'd gone through every possible scenario. The most obvious was that Fred's cover had been blown, and he'd been betrayed by his fellow spies, or by the Germans themselves. He'd risked his life doing something terribly dangerous, like breaking into a munitions factory or listening in on conversations between German military high command. He'd been mistaken for a German not just by other Germans but by someone on the other side, who didn't know there was an Allied spy working among the enemy, so he was killed as a German. I thought this was probably the most likely explanation.

The one possibility that never entered my head was that there might be a woman involved. I mean, I've heard of those spy stories where men are lured into bed by women in order to spill state secrets at the height of their passion – though more unlikely pillow talk I could not imagine. But that was not Fred. That was as far from Fred as it was possible to get. If I knew anything about my late husband, I knew he was not a philanderer. Never in the time I'd known him had he looked at another woman, or shown interest in them in any way. He was not that sort of man.

32

I arrived at the teahouse at five minutes to four to find every table taken up by a couple, or a group, except for one. Sitting on her own, in the corner facing the door, was a woman. She saw me right away and in the ten seconds or so that it took her to cross the room towards me, smiling, I realised that all my projections had been completely wrong. Of course. She was The Woman, K's wife, or lover, and Fred had fallen for her and she had betrayed him. You could see it in her eyes, they were very, very dark, like deep tunnels. She was a born seducer, a professional, even Fred couldn't resist . . .

'Mrs de Vere.' She held out her hand. It felt like a business meeting and I was about to be interviewed for a job. I shook her hand and did my best to smile back.

'Please.' She led me over to her table and sat me down opposite her. 'Tea?'

'Yes,' I said. 'Strong, no sugar.'

She beckoned to a waitress and placed the order.

I couldn't take my eyes off her. I've never met a seductress before, not a professional one. She had one of those Grecian-style faces with a distinguished nose that on someone less imposing would look ugly, but in her case it was all of a piece. Her eyes were hooded, as if her eyelids were so heavy she could barely lift them. She was Cleopatra, dark hair, eyes, complexion, everything.

'Where are you from?' I asked her.

'Serbia.' Now that was a surprise. I had to think for a moment whose side they'd been on in the war.

'And your name is Anna?'

She nodded. 'You can call me that.'

She wore deep scarlet lipstick, and fingernails to match. There were traces of red on the rim of the cup she was nursing and I idly wondered why someone who was a spy would leave such obvious traces of herself in such obvious places.

'I'm sorry it has taken me so long to get in contact with you.'

Her voice startled me for a moment.

'How did you find me?'

She gave me a lazy smile. 'I heard you were looking for information about your husband.'

'Did you know him?'

'Well, yes, and no.'

The waitress arrived with the tea and took what seemed to me to be a ridiculously long time placing the teapot carefully on the table, swivelling it so the handle was facing me, followed by the cup and saucer, the tiny jug of milk, and a teaspoon which she half dropped, merrily, into the saucer, before straightening up, looking at us both in turn and saying, 'Will there be anything else, madam?' to me, and then, 'Madam?' to my companion. And when we shook our heads and she finally turned and walked away I repeated the question:

'Did you know Fred?'

I poured my tea while the woman called Anna took a sip of hers and looked away for a moment. I imagined she was slipping back to that night in the seedy hotel in Berlin – no, Brussels – just her and him and the crumpled sheets and the sound of artillery fire in the distance.

'He was working for my husband.' She turned back to

look at me. The smile had gone now.

'Your husband is K?'

'Was.'

'I see.' I was right about one thing at least.

'My husband was Dutch/Belgian,' she went on. 'He was a tailor by trade and he got involved in espionage quite by accident. He happened to be in the right place at the right time, you could say.' She looked down at the table. 'Or you could say the wrong place at the wrong time.'

'Go on.'

'It is a long story,' she began. She placed her cup back into its saucer with great care.

'My husband was a tailor as I said, and he used to travel many distances to see his customers before the war so it was not unusual for him to be away from home.'

She wasn't looking at me. In another world, I thought, we might have had a lot in common. Wives of spies.

'He was not a man who – stood out. He was good at his job, very . . .' she searched for the right word, 'precise.' She jabbed the tablecloth with her fingernail to emphasise her point. 'Very good memory, very good brain. Yes. All this. This is what they wanted, I imagine. Spies are not remarkable men.' She looked up at me then. 'I don't need to tell you that.'

She did not need to tell me that.

'He had always been an easy-going sort of fellow, very relaxed, never anxious, always reassuring. Whereas I . . .' She laughed, briefly. 'We had a good marriage, until the war came. As I said, I am from Serbia so the Germans were our enemies, our – how do you say it – arch enemies. I hated them.'

She spoke mildly, almost mockingly.

'On the other hand my husband did not. He said they were people just like us, and I told him that might be so but their leaders were still animals. Look what they did to the Belgians! He agreed, of course, but still.' She leaned towards me conspiratorially. 'He was just appeasing me you see, he was always appeasing me.' She sighed.

'So you can imagine, when the war broke out, here I am, a Serbian living in Holland, a neutral country. But I was not neutral. Not in any way. I wanted to see the Germans . . .' She made a gesture as if swatting a fly, with surprising violence. 'I told him he should do something and he said, "Like what?" And I said, "I don't know, you speak Dutch and French, that must be something," and he said, "What, you think I should become a spy?"'

She laughed.

'So he became a spy because of you?'

The woman called Anna shrugged. 'Who knows? Perhaps. He certainly didn't seem to have strong feelings about the war, or the Germans, not like me. But he did so much for me.'

'He became a spy to please you, is that what you're saying?'

'I have no idea. I never asked him.' She was playing with her teaspoon, her eyes on the spoon, her mind elsewhere.

'So,' she said sharply, replacing the spoon on the saucer. 'It was my birthday, an important one you could say, if such things are ever important. We were going to celebrate at a little place nearby but at the last minute he told me he was very sorry, but he had to be elsewhere.'

She was careful never to mention his name, I noticed.

'This was . . .' She threw her hands in the air. 'This was very unusual, it had never happened before! It was not like him. But then, what could I do? And after that, it was never the same. He was not . . . no longer the husband I had known. He was anxious. No, not anxious. He was . . .'

'Preoccupied?'

'Pardon me? Yes, preoccupied. And you know, it is a strange thing, that you can notice a change but you don't always . . .' she sucked in her cheeks, 'you don't say anything, you don't do anything, and when you look back you think – Why didn't I?'

I nodded. It was taking a while and I didn't want to interrupt her unnecessarily.

'I should have, I would have, of course.'

I was wondering whether she was ever going to get beyond these wretched self-examinations.

'The thing is, they explained to me later, they had asked him, since he spoke the languages, to be their liaison. Their . . .' another gesture, 'coordinator, the person who organised the agents working under him. He was the only one who knew who they were. They worked separately, in cells, so nobody knew what the others were doing. It was safer that way.' She paused.

'Yes?' I prompted.

'Your husband was one of those agents, working under my husband so to speak. They told me he was rather special.'

'Who told you?'

She made another vague gesture. 'He was embedded among the enemy.'

'I knew that.'

'He was working behind a bar, did you know that?'

I shook my head.

'He became very friendly with some of the German soldiers who came into the bar. He was one of them. Nobody suspected him, not for a moment, nobody questioned. As my husband would say, they were regular soldiers, regular men, decent men – well, some of them. Not all of them, of course.'

'Was that where he was when he died? Behind the bar?'

She started playing with her teaspoon again. Meanwhile my tea was growing cold, I was too on edge to drink it.

'Mrs de Vere I did not know all this until later, much later. At the time I began to suspect my husband was having an affair. His change of behaviour, his being away so much, sometimes he would leave the house without a moment's notice. "I will be back in no time, Anna!" Then he'd be gone for days, and no explanation after. There was no time, you see. He was so busy. So very, very busy. A *tailor*, in the war. What could keep him so busy?

'I asked him, of course, I said, "Why is it you go so suddenly? Where are you going?" And he answered something about uniforms, he was being asked to make uniforms.' She pulled a face. 'These things are made in factories, did he think I was stupid? So I followed him. I thought he had an assignation – I thought it must be with a lady, what else? But it was not, it was with a man, so I thought . . .' She stopped.

'You thought?'

'An assignation with a man!' She snorted. 'Who? Why? What for? So I confronted him. *Them*. I confronted them. I didn't know what else to do. I said, "What is going on here?" and my husband – my *husband* – told me it was none of my business. This is impossible! Never did he speak to me in that way before.'

'Was that man my husband?'

'Oh no, he was just one of my husband's agents, one of his messengers, I imagine. They all passed messages, that's what they did, in code, and the code changed all the time. I don't know what the messages were saying, perhaps they were about the travelling of German troops, yes, that's what I think they were. People would watch the trains, different people in different places, and makes notes about them.'

'That's all very well.' I was beginning to run out of patience. 'What did all that have to do with my husband?'

'Your husband was behind enemy lines.'

'You said that already. I knew that already. You haven't yet told me anything I didn't already know.'

She looked at me, startled by my ferocity.

'Just tell me what happened. In one paragraph.'

'Very well.' She took a deep breath. 'You haven't drunk your tea.'

'Just tell me.'

'Of course. Well. When I found out my husband was having assignations with these people, I tried to stop him.'

'Why?'

'Why? Because . . . I just did not want him to have assignations, I did not want him to be doing things I didn't know about, that's all. That's all it was. I promise.'

'But you're the one who encouraged him in the first place. To be a spy. Isn't that what you said?'

She wrinkled her brow. 'Maybe. But when it came to it, I . . .'

I waited.

'I couldn't stand it! I did not trust him. I could not stand him having a secret life. It makes no sense perhaps, but that's the way it was.'

There was a pause. She was frowning into her teacup.

'So?'

'So the next time he said he had to go somewhere I pretended to be ill. Very ill. Terrible stomach cramps.' She clutched her abdomen, by way of demonstration.

'I was screaming. He said he had to go, he would look for a doctor while he was out. I said there were no doctors, they were all far too busy, he must stay with me. He must stay with me.' She thumped the tablecloth and the teacups rattled. 'I held onto him – I've never done such a thing in my life – I held onto him and said things like, "What if I'm
208

dying, what if you come back and find me dead, right here on the bed? What of that?" And he was alarmed, of course, he was in great turmoil. He said to me, "I have to go out, it's vitally important," and I said to him, "What can possibly be so important that you desert your dying wife?"'

She let out a sudden laugh, and stifled it as suddenly.

'So, I stopped him. In the end, he was struggling, but he stayed. And when I could see he wasn't going anywhere I calmed down.' She thought for a moment. 'The following day came the news that the bar your husband was working in . . .'

'Yes?'

'Was destroyed by the Allies. Everyone killed. Around thirty of them, I believe.'

There was a silence. I could not speak.

'And your husband was with them. The message did not get through to inform the British that there was an Allied agent working there. So they bombed the bar. Your husband was destroyed by his own people. He was destroyed,' she took a handkerchief from her pocket and dabbed at her nose, 'by me.'

There it was then. Destroyed by friends. Betrayed by a woman, but not in the way I had thought.

'I did not mean to do harm. I was simply – jealous. Insecure.' Her voice had dropped to a near whisper. 'If I had known, if I had had any idea of what might happen . .
'

I didn't know what to say. There was nothing to say. There was nothing.

'My husband was killed very soon after that. Shot trying to get through the border into France. I didn't hear about it until much later, after the war was over.' She sniffled, blew her nose and scrunched the handkerchief in her hand. 'It wasn't until then that they told me what he'd been doing. He was a vital agent, that's what they called him. A crucial link in the chain. He was the chain. He was the one who held everything together. And I broke the chain and destroyed him.'

'I can't see how you work that out.'

'I destroyed him because I would not let him leave the house. I no longer trusted him. He no longer trusted me. Had he trusted me he would have told me. Not everything, but enough. I might not have liked it, I might have tried to stop him, I *would* have tried to stop him in fact, he knew that, which is why he did not tell me. And because he did not tell me, everything went wrong. Everything. Because I would not let him leave the house, the chain was broken. Messages did not get through. Communications were lost. People were in the wrong place, not where they should be. It was such a tight . . .' she balled her fists together, 'network. Everyone relying on everyone else. You break the chain and it all goes wrong.'

I didn't know who she was grieving for most, her husband or herself. Or perhaps, just perhaps, Fred.

'So that's the story of how your husband died.'

She was obviously expecting a barrage of something or other. But I was still in the process of absorbing everything.

'Would you like a fresh cup of tea?' she asked me gently.

I shook my head.

'Thank you for telling me,' I said. 'It can't have been easy.'

'It was not easy. I have not told anyone else. I left everyone to think it was a mistake. That the Allies did not know about your husband, which is true, they did not, but they should have. I let them think the fault was theirs, which is bad of me.'

'Well, I don't suppose it matters a huge deal.'

That was a faintly idiotic thing to say in the circumstances. A man dies, so what? Does it really matter how? This poor woman, I felt for her.

'Is there anything else you need to know?'

I thought for a long while about this. In the end all I could come up with was, 'What was my husband doing working in a bar?'

'I don't know. I imagine it was because it was the perfect place. He was able to pick up the gossip and pass it on.'

'I see.' I did and I did not. I could not picture Fred as a barman. He was a non-drinker for a start, or he was until he met me. I put paid to that, or tried to.

So there was the truth, the facts: Fred blown to bits along with his German pals, and I'm sure they were pals, he must have got to know them pretty well. That can't have been easy either, to know you're spying on your pals. What a nasty, hateful business it all was.

'If it helps you to know, I have terrible sleepless nights.'

'I'm sorry to hear it,' I muttered.

'I don't say this to make you pity me. I say it because it is on my conscience. Two men, who died, on my conscience.'

'It was war after all,' I managed to reply. 'Everything was a mess in the war. It must have happened to many people. Mistakes. Miscommunications. Must have.'

I sat there for another minute or so. There should have been things I wanted to know, questions I wanted to ask, but I couldn't think of a thing. So I suddenly got up to go.

'If you need to get hold of me for anything.' She was holding out a card with her name on it. I looked at her face and it was wet, she was crying. I took the card, nodded at her briefly and left.

It was good to get into the fresh air. I hadn't realised

how much I was suffocating in that tiny café with its steamed-up windows.

~

The story as I related it to Sacha later that evening did not make total sense. At least, he didn't think it did.

'But,' he kept interjecting, 'you mean she did all that out of *jealousy*? Why didn't he tell her? Why did he let her push him around like that?' I told him spies *never* talked about what they did, even to their nearest and dearest, he knew that from what I'd told him of Fred.

'It's ironic,' said Sacha, 'that he only became a spy in the first place because of her. To please her, or to appease her, as you say. You'd think she would have put two and two together, wouldn't you?'

'What do you mean?'

'Well, you'd think she would have twigged that's what he was doing. Hence the secrecy.' He shrugged. 'I guess I will never fully understand the workings of the female mind.'

I tried to put myself in her position. What would I have done? I gave up after a few seconds.

Sacha looked thoughtful. 'So,' he said, 'is that satisfying, Rudi? Can you put it all behind you now?'

I said the part that worried me the most – no, not worried, perplexed me rather – was imagining Fred behind a bar. I never saw him pour a drink in his life, that was my job. To be truthful I never *let* him pour a drink, he had no idea how to do it. His dry martinis were a travesty despite hours of painstaking instruction. Nor did he ever really take to drinking himself, despite my encouragement.

Yet that was how he had spent his time in the war and that was how he had died. Pouring drinks for Germans. Friendly Germans. Germans resting and relaxing between bombing raids, forgetting their cares, forgetting about the war, getting drunk. Fred as a barman.

'What are you thinking, Rudi?'

'I'm thinking, I hope Fred had a few drinks inside him when he died. And I hope it was quick. It would have been quick, wouldn't it, Sacha? He wouldn't have known anything.'

'He wouldn't have known a thing, Rudi,' said Sacha, and gave me a big hug.

~

That night I lay awake pondering the gaps and the background to Anna's story.

There were questions I should have asked her, but I didn't think of them till later. Why, for instance, had it taken so long, like a whole eight years, for her to get in touch with me? And how had she managed to get the full story when I couldn't? And why should I believe it anyway? She had nothing to gain from making the whole thing up, far from it, but on the other hand . . . Oh what the hell, I thought, I was too tired to care, and what details she wasn't able to tell me I could very well make up myself, and so I did.

When war broke out Fred, or Hans as he was known, was posing as a tutor at Heidelberg University. I had no idea where Heidelberg was, but he had been a student there in his youth. When his students were called up he found himself out of a job and drifting, and the drifting took him into this cosy bar in D, a small town not far from the city of M, where a contingent of German troops happened to be stationed, and this bar was where they drank of an evening.

It so happened that on the day of Hans' first visit the bar was without its barman, who had also been called up. The locals had taken it in turns to do the job in his stead, but as the evenings wore on so the more they drank and the more inattentive they became so the takings in the till bore no relation to the drink that had been consumed. In a fit of enthusiasm Fred, or Hans, volunteered his services, even though he freely confessed he'd never poured a drink in his life before, but he could add up and he was honest, he assured them. That's how Fred, or Hans, became a barman.

He quite enjoyed the job, to his surprise, and as a non-drinker he stayed sober throughout all those long boozy evenings, which meant not only did the till tally at the end of each heavy drinking session but he was able to obtain vital snippets of information from the clientele. He knew when a certain platoon was to be sent to a certain place, he even knew what ships were in harbour at any particular time at B, the nearest sea port, not far away. Once the bar was closed and the men had gone back to barracks he retired to his lonely room, where he carefully wrote out all he had learned that evening, in code, ready to be passed on to the Special Messenger the following day. The Special Messenger being the most unlikely person of Frau Frauleiner.

Frau Frauleiner was a fat, middle-aged and unbeautiful soul with a secret past. She came from Switzerland and she had once been an exotic dancer of humble origins who'd married a German aristocrat for his money. But he had treated her abominably and, on his early death (from failure of the liver) she discovered he had left her with nothing. For reasons of revenge on the entire German race she had turned spy during the war and, while keeping up a front as a plump, homely widow with too many cats, she spied for the Allies.

Fond of schnapps, Frau Frauleiner would drop into the bar for a snifter or two at lunchtime, usually when the German soldiers were not around. She would enjoy a bit of chitchat with Hans the barman who would pass on to her, along with her change, little slips of paper with code on them, which she in turn would pass on to the baker's son, a lad just turned fifteen, who passed them on to who knows who, and so on down the line until they reached the happy hands of K. K and Fred/Hans had never actually met but they felt they knew one another intimately.

All this worked tremendously well for a year. No one had the slightest suspicion about Hans/Fred, and when anyone asked him if he had a family he said regretfully no, he had not yet found the woman of his dreams but he was quite happy living on his own and was by now quite used to it and not in the least lonely. And forgive him if he didn't invite anyone into his garret because quite frankly, *liebe Herren,* they would not want to set foot into such a pigsty.

He was popular among the German soldiers, mostly because he was such a good listener, and since he was not one of them they felt able to sound off to him about their commanding officers and their ridiculous plans to send them to X when they knew they should be going to Y. They also told him about their girlfriends, and on occasion their boyfriends, and their stories sometimes made his hair stand on end and sometimes made him feel quite weepy.

It wasn't easy getting this close to all these young men, knowing that many of them were going to meet their demise on their next sortie, and that his work would help them on their way. But he comforted himself by thinking of the girl he had left back home, and how much her future depended on defeating the Hun and how proud she would be if she knew of the vital part he had played in the victory. It was the thought of returning home to his beloved wife that kept him going, and the sooner he could make that happen, which meant the quicker he and the rest of them could send the enemy packing, the better.

The evening the bomb fell was like any other. The bar

was packed. Juergen the Playboy was there, as was Fritz the Moustache and Moritz the Knee – so called because he slapped it while playing the accordion, to the annoyance of his fellow soldiers. Hans was in his place behind the bar thinking of his wife and imagining her there beside him, looking on at the cheerful carryings-on and joining in the singing. She had the voice of a nightingale, he had told her on more than one occasion. She was a remarkable woman in every way and the longer he spent away from her, the more he missed her. He reminded himself to tell her the next time he saw her what a wonderful woman she was and how lucky he was to have found her, and if it hadn't been for that little mishap with the heel and the grill at Paddington station – or was it Euston? how could he have forgotten? – his life would have meant nothing, nothing at all.

When he got home the first thing he would do is take her beautiful, softly rounded body in his arms and bury his face in her hair – that 'frizz', as she insisted on calling it – which he loved, because it smelt of spices and lemon and sometimes faintly of lard. He would feel the warmth of her body spreading throughout him and he would tell himself he was the luckiest man in the world.

It was a direct hit. It was said that at the moment the bomb exploded the soldiers were in full song, that Fritz the Moustache was showing off his fandango and Moritz his knee-slap, and the barman, along with the others, died with a smile on his face.

It was silly, but it helped. I slept for the rest of the night, also with a smile on my face.

33

I did a lot of thinking after that, and I came to the eventual and shocking conclusion that my beloved husband had got his just deserts.

Assuming, as I did, that he had made friends with those German soldiers, how could he have stood back and watched them being blown to pieces by an Allied bomb? Knowing that he was responsible for all those deaths? Or if not directly responsible, at the very least implicated. It's one thing to pass on enemy secrets and quite another to pretend to be one of the people you are betraying.

It didn't fit with Fred's personality at all, which made it all the harder to comprehend. I doubt he had ever knowingly offended anyone in his life. He was perhaps the most inoffensive person I ever came across, as Sacha had more than once pointed out. Everybody liked Fred; he had a friendly, unthreatening demeanour which made other people relax in his company, knowing he was not their rival or out to steal their wife or their money. He was just – Fred.

And yet as I saw it, my husband had done more actual harm in the end than anyone else I knew. Putting aside for one moment the bomb that killed him and his pals, how many other young men had gone to their deaths because of him? There was absolutely no use telling me he was working for us, against the enemy, doing his utmost to help to win and therefore to end that terrible war. That he was a hero, sacrificing his safety and ultimately his life for the cause. I could not see beyond the people, those innocent soldiers who by dint of where they were born happened to be our enemy. Not because they were bad people or murdered people for kicks or did anything else that made them unsavoury; just because they were foreigners. Men like our men, with the same urges and longings, young men to boot, following orders from generals they'd never met, at war for reasons they weren't privy to.

Nothing could shift me. Nothing that Sacha said could alter my mind. Fred was a liar. Spies are liars and cheats. There is nothing glamorous about being a spy. It is a cowardly way to spend your time, by eavesdropping and pretending, and hiding behind a false front. If Fred could convince German soldiers he was one of them, who else did he dupe into believing he was other than who he was? Including his wife.

These thoughts rankled, and kept me awake, and while I knew in my heart of hearts that to me Fred was exactly who he said he was, I also knew he was a cheat and a liar. And in a weird kind of a way that helped to close the door on the whole unhappy mess.

My thoughts mellowed as time went on. That's the strange thing about thoughts, they'll lead you in all sorts of unexpected directions if you let them. Sacha told me my thoughts were my survival instincts, that the tosh I was coming out with at the time was my way of coping with Fred's death – which is true, of course, but doesn't mean they were wrong. Sacha then had the effrontery to add that Fred had suddenly become interesting, and how sorry he was that it was too late to get to know him better. He also said, paradoxically, that it was Fred's common decency which meant he could not have lived with himself after the war, knowing what he had done. 'Put like that, you could say the same about everyone who fought in the war and survived it,' I said, waspishly. At which point my brain could take no more and decided to shut down completely.

~

Earlier in the year, I had booked myself on a trip to Italy to study Renaissance art – not, I hasten to add, because of any particular interest in the Old Masters so much as an excuse to get out and away from my four walls and play the Merry Widow Abroad.

It was a role I had perfected, if I say it myself. Since I am not the sort of woman that other men's wives consider a threat, I have always been able to laugh and flirt with those other men to my heart's content. They were usually pretty bored, having only come on the trip in the first place for the food, or the pretty Italian women, and because their spouses insisted. So I considered it my duty to the long-suffering wives to draw the attention of the men away from the lovely signorinas – who were, let's face it, out of bounds for men of that age – and onto something slightly closer to home.

But on this occasion I found I no longer had the heart for it. I felt Fred was there, looking over my shoulder and laughing at me in his sardonic way. Usually ghosts only appear when they're not laid to rest, so the saying goes, but Fred had been laid to rest quite firmly, so what was he doing chuckling into my ear?

I made my usual merry jokes, about the fat-bottomed, flat-bosomed goddesses of the Renaissance, but every time I tried to flirt a bit there was Fred, looking on. I did manage one brief liaison with one of the bored husbands in the cocktail hour, when his wife had retired for a pre-dinner nap, but even that failed to raise my spirits much.

Our guide, Pierre, was what in the past I'd have

described as a middle-aged woman's dream. He was raffishly handsome, and as learned as he was unworldly. He may have known everything there was to know about Renaissance women, but nothing whatsoever about the 1920s lasses who surrounded him. He took not the blindest bit of notice of the beautiful, black-eyed signorinas who brushed so very accidentally against him in the galleries or fluttered their eyelashes at him over their espressos. He could be passionate about a near-naked Botticelli, but I don't suppose he'd seen the real thing in the flesh in his entire life. Innocence shone out of him like a beacon, and in normal circumstances I would have homed in on Pierre with the deadly focus of a Springfield rifle. But on this occasion something held me back.

'Goddammit Fred,' I found myself saying, 'you've done for me.'

34

I'd barely stepped over the threshold on my return to Pimlico when Claudia was on the telephone, sounding decidedly flustered. 'Darling,' she said to me, 'have I got news for you!'

Needless to say I pretended not to be *too* interested, but I did promise after a reasonable chance to catch my breath to drive down to Hallywell to see her. It was, in truth, exactly what I needed: a few days in the countryside with my closest friend, who despite being my closest friend had barely known Fred. I determined not to mention his name all the time I was there, in the hope that by ignoring him completely he would lose interest in us and bugger off.

It was a week or so before I arrived on the Faradays' doorstep, Rosie panting and wheezing like an old mother hen with emphysema, by which time Claudia had recovered her composure. I did as I always did, and immediately launched into the tale of my recent adventures in Tuscany, embroidered on this occasion for Claudia's sake. It was always worth it for the look on her face.

This time was different, however. As a rule when I'm rabbiting away Claudia will sit stock still, expressionless, and only the sharp-eyed would notice her face growing paler, and the wince – no, more of a tic than a wince – in the corner of her mouth as the embellishments spill forth.

After a while she will start to shake her head, and with a flutter of her hands plead, 'No more, that's enough, thank you.'

I do not, by the way, usually go into physical detail about my exploits with men, with Claudia or with anyone. But on this occasion I was skimming through my little fling with Signor Martini (the husband of the wife with the pre-dinner nap), exaggerated to suit the occasion, when she stopped me and started asking questions: how long did it take, what did we do, exactly, where were we, where was Signora Martini all the while, and so on.

'You want *details*?' You could have knocked me down with the proverbial feather. She claimed she did. And so I told her what she wanted to know, all the time watching her face fill with distaste. The more I told her, the more sickened she looked until I thought she might throw up right there on the carpet in front of us. And yet she did not let up. It was the oddest thing and led me to believe that Claudia was Up To Something.

That Something must have had to do with Dougie. Later that evening she told me everything: how he'd telephoned her out of the blue a couple of weeks ago and suggested dinner in Town. She had been planning a trip to see Jess and Jonno anyway at their place in Primrose Hill, and while she was there she'd spent an evening with Dougie and heard his story. He'd been working overseas apparently, and been married, not too happily, and lost his only son in the war. His wife had died, and now he'd come back to live in London and write books. Then as he was walking her back to Primrose Hill from the little restaurant off Oxford Street, he'd propositioned her. 'Just one night,' he'd pleaded.

Dougie was the one who was always expected to marry Claudia, if you remember, and from that day to this neither I nor anyone else was ever able to explain why she turned him down in favour of the wretched Gerald. Even Gerald had been taken by surprise.

Claudia appeared to see things differently. I really wonder about that woman sometimes. She seemed surprised when I told her how desperately in love with her Dougie had always been. She didn't even have a proper explanation for marrying Gerald, except to say, without much conviction, that she loved him. I told her Dougie had loved her all his life, then and now, and if she had a head on her shoulders she should go ahead and give him his night, and others, as many as they wanted. Besides, he was a wonderful lover.

Oops.

That did it.

She was out of the room before you could say Jack Rabbit. Then she wouldn't speak to me, that evening or the following day. So I had spent a night with Dougie, to comfort him on her behalf I could have added, but did not. And now Claudia was jealous, of *me*.

Claudia's problem, one of the many, is that she doesn't like sex. You can see it in the flinch, or the wince or the tic, whenever the subject arises. She is not alone there, there are many women of my acquaintance who think sex is the devil, or worse, a waste of time. It is a product of their Victorian upbringing, something I was lucky to bypass.

I told Claudia as much, not for the first time. She lapsed into sulky silence, also not for the first time, and remained that way for the rest of my prolonged stay. Prolonged I have to say due to a near collision between Rosie and a tractor on a blind corner the afternoon I arrived. Why country people think they own the road just because they drive a bigger vehicle is beyond me. Give me city driving any time. We were on our way to take tea in some godforsaken village in the middle of nowhere and ended up in a ditch instead, Rosie, me and Claudia, with no bones broken but a nasty dent in Rosie's front bit. So I was stuck at Hallywell for an extra day or two while Rosie went in for repairs.

It wasn't until I was on my way home in my spanking, gleaming car – and no longer wheezing, I noticed – that I had a sudden thought about Claudia.

Being the self-centred creature that I am, it hadn't struck me at the time, but there was definitely something different about Claudia. Her clothes, for a start. Someone had got at her, taken her out of her Victorian garb and put her into something almost up-to-date. Shorter hems, looser bodices – they suited her, I have to admit.

But there was something else about Claudia, something less definable. Her strange attachment to an ancient oak tree in the grounds of the house. Her eagerness to hear details of my sexual exploits in Italy. Her reaction to my sleeping with Dougie.

There was only one possible cause: Claudia had a lover.

Incredible though it seemed, she'd been ravished, and she'd enjoyed it.

But if so, who by?

35

I heard nothing from Claudia for a while after that. Nor did I pursue her. It's the way things go with friends. You fall out, you wonder why you were friends in the first place, you fall back in. Life goes on. Whatever it was she was up to, I would find out sooner or later.

Then I bumped into Dougie. It was at dinner at the house of mutual friends of ours from way back, a reunion of the carefree empty-headed creatures of our youth. They'd known Claudia, of course, and Gerald. Dougie was his usual dapper self. Thirty years on but still trim, still with hair, still bounding up the steps of the house like a youngster.

He told us about his adventures in far-off lands, working for the Foreign Office as a diplomat, 'flying the flag for good old England'. There were entertaining stories of the people he'd met in those remote corners of Asia and Australia, where he and his colleagues hunkered down in 'little pockets of England', growing roses in Ceylon and eating porridge in Sydney, to the amusement of the locals. He'd fought in the war but didn't want to talk about it. Married, but didn't seem to want to talk about that either. Lost his only son in the war. It hadn't been the best of lives and only Dougie could make it all sound like one long lark.

Claudia's name was conspicuous by its absence from

our conversation. Dougie never mentioned her and because of this nor did I. Even I can hold my tongue if necessary. The more we ignored her existence, the more of a solid entity she became, as if she were sitting at the table right next to us.

I asked Dougie what his plans were and he said he was looking to settle in London.

'And do what?' I enquired.

'Write books.'

'*Books*?' I exclaimed. 'Whatever for? What makes you think you're a writer? Are you expecting to make a living?'

He laughed and said he didn't mind, he just wanted to write whatever came into his head. His thoughts, his reminiscences, stories from his life, a romance maybe.

'A romance?'

'Dearest Prudence,' he said, quite fondly, I thought. 'Do I disgust you so much?'

'You don't disgust me at all, Dougie,' I told him. 'How could you disgust anyone? It's just I can't see the point of being a writer. Sitting there day after day, on your own, scribble scribble scribble, while all sorts of things are going on outside your very window.'

I asked him where he was living, at which he pulled a face and said he was staying with his sister. It wasn't ideal, he went on. In fact it was getting decidedly less ideal the longer he stayed there, so he was planning on renting a place somewhere as soon as he could find the time to look.

'The time to tear yourself away from your pen and paper,' I said, with as much sarcasm as I could muster.

'That's about right,' he responded genially.

Dear Dougie, insult him how you may he never takes offence. So I found myself saying, 'You can come and stay with me if you like. Until you find somewhere else.'

'I don't suppose so,' he responded, still smiling. 'Thanks all the same, old girl.'

I wasn't fond of the 'old girl'.

I shrugged. 'Just trying to help. You could have the spare room and use it as a study, scribble away to your heart's content all day. I won't disturb you.'

'And have to put up with your jibes, you mean?'

'No jibes, I promise.' I smiled back at him with both my faces. 'The offer is there.'

And the offer was accepted. A week later, Dougie moved into my spare room.

~

It was not a peaceful life with Dougie as my guest. He made a point of disappearing into his room straight after breakfast and not emerging until midday. He bought himself a typewriter which I could hear clattering away, then we'd share a spot of lunch together and on occasion we'd go out and walk around a bit until the light began to fade. Then he'd go back into his room for a while though I didn't hear the typewriter so I imagine he was napping.

There were some monumental rows. He broke one of my best Spodes once, all because he mocked me for never having heard of some obscure writer who he thought I ought to know, so I threw a plate at him. He loved it. It became a game, a childish one, but fun.

Then one day over lunch he confessed what I could have told him from the start: he was not a writer.

'After all that,' he said ruefully, 'I don't seem to have anything to say.'

I said he had plenty to say, it was just the way he was going about it.

'Conversation is all very well Prue, but . . .' He took a breath. 'You see, I'd rather like to be remembered by posterity. Conversations come and go, but books go on forever. And in the end, I'm not sure my life has been that interesting.'

I told him he should make it up, exaggerate if

necessary. It was perfectly easy, I did it all the time.

'Then maybe I should write your story,' he said.

'No fear!' I told him. 'If anyone's going to write my story it's going to be me.'

It was one of the more ridiculous things I've said in my life. Me who's barely even read a book.

But you know, I did. Or rather I made the notes, clumsy and incoherent, and passed them on to Dougie. And he, well, he made some kind of sense of it all, insofar as my life makes sense in the first place. My life.

~

It took us a while to get around to telling Claudia that Dougie and I were cohabiting, and when we did, her face was a picture. I could see she was both appalled and curious, and even slightly jealous. She didn't know what to make of it. I could see she was dying to ask The Question: *Are you sleeping together*? but she couldn't do it, and we were not going to tell her. Dougie enjoyed the deception as much as I did. He has a deliciously catty side to him that I was not previously aware of.

We were not sleeping together. I know I appear to have no scruples but when it came to Dougie and Claudia, I drew the line. No matter she was married to someone else, Dougie belonged to Claudia, if he belonged to anyone. He told me very firmly that she had rejected him yet again, and I eventually heard on the grapevine that she and Gerald had become reconciled and she'd gone to live with him in Palestine or somewhere, so really there was nothing to stop me. To stop us. And yet we abstained.

After a month or so of living together Dougie said it was time for him to leave and stand on his own two feet, like a proper grown-up. There was a little place in Shepherd's Bush he had his eye on, 'not very salubrious, Prue, but I hope you'll come and visit me there one day.'

I said I had no intention of visiting him in Shepherd's

Bush or anywhere else for that matter. He was not going anywhere.

Surprising though it may sound, I'd got used to having him around. I'd even grown fond of the arguments and the plate-throwing. I loved to see Dougie riled. He was very rarely riled but when he was, it was a joy to behold. After one particular session he said something to me I'll never forget.

'It may astonish you to hear this, Prue, but you make me feel more alive than I've felt since I was a young man.'

'So you're staying?'

'I suppose I am,' he said.

And he did.

Finale

So there it is, the story of my life so far. You may well think it was hardly worth putting down on paper. I don't doubt that anyone expecting the tell-all memoirs of a good-time girl has been mightily disappointed.

I did find purpose, but not perhaps as Sacha or the rest of the world thinks of it, with a capital P. Purpose in my experience is a temporary thing that changes from day to day.

There's been the purpose of finding out about and enjoying sex. And while Claudia may have found a new lease of life at the age of fifty-something, her slightly younger if more world-weary friend is thinking of putting all that behind her. Though you never know, there's a lot of life in the old dog yet.

There was the purpose of getting to know Mrs Pat – Stella – who played a more influential role in my life than she could ever have imagined, and a more lasting one than she ever played on stage. I followed her life and career in the newspapers. Her husband was killed in the Boer War and she married again, a Major George Cornwall-West, whose first wife was Lady Randolph, Winston Churchill's mother. However Stella is far better known for her relationship with the writer George Bernard Shaw, who worshipped the ground she walked on, as did we all. She is still going strong as I write this, and one of these days I intend to pitch up at her stage door as I did all those years ago and tell her how much I owe her.

Then there were the suffragists, the personification of purpose. I have fond memories of those dear, distraught, well-bred ladies, into whose hearts, I like to think, I planted the seeds of civil disobedience. They finally got their way, at least partly, after the war ended, and I've no doubt in time they'll achieve their full purpose. If it's true, as some unkind people have said, that they would have achieved their purpose anyway after the war ended, that means their purpose was ultimately purposeless. It ignores all those brave souls who were imprisoned and force-fed, only to be released if they were ill and then re-arrested once they were well again under something quaintly known as the Cat and Mouse Act. Not to mention the martyr Emily Davison, killed by King George V's horse during the Derby. If I never quite managed to achieve anything like the suffragists' sense of purpose I can only blame my short attention span.

I did find purpose during the war. I make no bones about the reason for doing what I did, which was entirely selfish. There has never been anything to raise the adrenaline and blood count quicker than driving at speed without lights down an unfamiliar road in the blackout. Nothing has ever really come close to that level of excitement, before or since. In another life perhaps I could have become a racing driver.

Fred was my purpose too, in a completely different sense. I'm not good at love. I was brought up without knowing what it was, and as the saying goes, what you don't know you don't miss. The words 'I love you' are banded about so carelessly these days, partly in order for the male of the species to encourage the female of the species into bed. Stella aside, I don't believe I ever told anyone I loved them. I'm not even sure, looking back, that

I said those words to Fred. I think he knew. I hope he did. Because I did love him, I just don't remember getting around to saying it. I'm not sure I'd have always loved him, who knows, but he was away an awful lot, which is a very clever way of keeping love alive. He still appears to me from time to time, when things are quiet or I'm not thinking of anything much, which is often. He's a comfort really, as he always was, like a warm blanket. And I'd rather like it if he stuck around. If telling a ghost you love him counts then I've achieved that small thing at least.

I do love Sacha, and Claudia of course, in my own way. And Dougie. If love means you miss a person when they're not there, and no matter how much you annoy the pants off one another you'd be genuinely sad if they died, or disappeared, then I guess I love all of them. This is me talking honestly, the woman who's always put herself first and never seriously considered other people's concerns before her own.

Talking of Sacha, he fetched up on my doorstep one afternoon wearing what I took to be a clown costume. I asked him if he'd become a children's entertainer and he looked pained and told me he'd joined the Dada movement, which as far as I can tell is a bunch of talentless people doing silly things for the sake of it. Typical of Sacha to latch onto the latest short-lived craze, and typical of me to pour scorn onto him for it. Some things never change and never will.

Sacha has finally found his soulmate in a strange-looking Hungarian boy called Eesop, or that's how it sounds. We met briefly one day in a Lyon's Corner House, which Eesop thought was the most beautiful place he had ever set foot in. He was five foot nothing with bandy legs and scraggy hair, not Sacha's type at all I wouldn't have thought, but he had boundless enthusiasm and even waxed eloquent about the pigeons in Trafalgar Square.

Whatever makes my dear Sacha happy.

As I write these words it's 1925, and I have reached my half century, a sobering thought. But I have twenty years ahead of me till I reach the Biblical allocation of three score years and ten, and that's a lot of time to fill for a woman with plenty of get-up-and-go left in her.

What's more the world is enjoying what they're calling the Roaring Twenties. There's jazz, and moving pictures, and wirelesses, and everywhere you look a feeling that anything is possible, anything goes. New clothes, new architecture, new everything. It's impossible not to get caught up in it. Call me shallow, but we've had enough of the dark days and there can only be lightness ahead, and fun, and who knows what sorts of ridiculous and unexpected things to enjoy.

In the meantime I will continue living with Dougie in our unique form of unmarried and unconsummated togetherness for however long we can survive without killing one another, or worse, boring one another. And if I have a purpose, or ever needed one, the continuing day-to-day astonishments of everyday life are enough. The moment they stop, then so do I.

As for what purpose I have served to the world, if any, I like to think I have entertained a few people, and made them laugh, if nothing more. And if you dear reader have stayed with me this far and I have managed to raise in you the odd smile, or even a tear, that's good enough for me.

Acknowledgements

Once again, a big thank you to Joan Deitch for her editing and encouragement.

§

If you enjoyed this book it would be delightful if you could post a review on the retail platform you bought it from. Thank you.

Author biography

Patsy Trench lives in London. Her previous books, about her family's history in Australia, are informal yet informative accounts of that country's early colonial beginnings. In a previous life she was an actress, scriptwriter, playscout, founder of *The Children's Musical Theatre of London* and lyricist. When not writing books she teaches theatre and organises theatre trips for overseas students. She is the mother of two grown-ups and grandmother of one, and her hobbies are rag rugging and mudlarking on the Thames foreshore.

Social media

Facebook: PatsyTrenchWriting
Substack: https://substack.com/@patsytrenchauthor
X/Twitter: @PatsyTrench
Instagram: claudiafaraday1920
Website: www.patsytrench.com